Mystery Myth and Mayhem

By Ben Woodard

Miller-Martin Press

Mystery, Myth, and Mayhem

Ben Woodard © 2019
All Rights Reserved

Middle Grade Short Stories

No portion of this book may be copied, transmitted, duplicated, stored, or distributed in any form (including, but not limited to print, mechanical, audio, handwriting, video, digital, or electronic means), except for brief excerpts used in reviews or commentaries, without prior express written permission from the publisher.

ISBN: 978-1-7331229-0-0 (paperback)
ISBN:978-1-7331229-1-7 (ebook)

Cover design and lettering by Concinnity by Erica Cook

Published by: Miller-Martin Press
Lexington, KY

To Lynda

Contents

Mystery Myth and Mayhem

The Z Team

Chapter One

The Explosion

Kaboom! The windows rattled and the desks shook. The students jumped at the explosive sound.

"What in the world was that?" asked Ms. Whipple, the teacher.

The fire alarm bells clanged and Ms. Whipple hollered above the din to the panicked students, "Everyone please stand and follow our fire escape procedure."

The teacher opened the door and the smell of smoke rolled into the room. The children filed out of the room with Ms. Whipple urging them on.

"Faster and scrunch down," said Ms. Whipple. "Exits are on your right."

The class spilled into the playground and went to their designated spot to wait for instructions. Other classes filled the playground, all standing in groups of murmuring, scared children.

The smoke swirled outside the school and settled on a hill, covering an old graveyard with haze.

Zoey could barely breathe from smoke and fear. What had happened? She had a bad feeling that she knew.

Fire trucks rolled into the parking area coming from every direction and firefighters poured out of their vehicles and ran into the school.

After an hour, they lumbered back out taking off their gear. The teachers and students got the go-ahead to return to their classrooms.

The smoke had cleared as they walked back through the hallways, but there were still a few firefighters around and the school had a faint smell of burning leaves.

The students sat down and Ms. Whipple explained what had happened. There had been an explosion in the science lab. Fortunately there were no flames, but the blast damaged much of the room and equipment, and produced a lot of smoke.

Mrs. Woods, the lab teacher, suspected someone had brought unapproved chemicals to the school.

None of the chemicals approved by the school would have caused an explosion.

All of the students and the teacher stared at Zoey. They knew about all the times she didn't follow the rules. She couldn't help it. Everything about this school was boring. Kinda dead, really. Zoey loved chemistry, but the official experiments were nothing but dull. What was wrong with trying an unusual experiment?

But now she wanted to crawl inside her desk. She knew she was in big trouble. Something had gone wrong. Terribly wrong.

She couldn't move. She knew she had to get up and go find out what happened, but her body felt as heavy as a Mack truck.

Why? She had followed the instructions in her older brother's chemistry set—well, except for that one little change.

Her stomach tightened and she felt like she couldn't breathe. She had only added a couple of safe chemicals from the lab to the ones she brought from home. It should have worked and Mrs. Woods never would have known since Zoey hid it in a cabinet.

The public address system crackled out an order, "Student Zoey Zimmer, please report to the principal's office immediately."

She knew she was doomed. This would be the final straw. No telling what her parents would do to her. She had been in trouble way too many times for her experiments.

She pushed herself up from her desk and stumbled toward the door. The hallway still had firefighters in full gear walking ahead of her.

Well, at least, she thought, I didn't destroy the whole school. Maybe it wasn't all that bad.

Zoey was going to find out that it was much worse than she could imagine.

Chapter Two

Lacy

She returned to her classroom after meeting with the principal and her parents.

They were not happy and through all the muttering and babbling, she thought she heard that she would never have any electronic devices ever again, and she probably wouldn't be allowed to leave the house until she was twenty-one.

She slumped in her seat as snotty-nose Lacy made a face at her. Oh, how she hated that girl. Miss-priss-perfect, who managed to do everything Zoey did, but got away with it. But, of course, Lacy had never blown up the science lab.

Nobody had ever done that.

But Lacy was up to something. Zoey stared at her as the girl pulled out several books and some papers and arranged them like a fort on her desk. Ms. Whipple had her back to the class.

Lacy reached in her desk and pulled out a smart phone. She placed it discreetly between the books and papers looking straight ahead all the time.

Texting, thought Zoey, that's what she's up to. It was against the rules to use a phone in school, but rules didn't apply to Lacy. She was the rich cheerleader who could do anything and her parents would never say a word. Life just wasn't fair.

As Zoey reached down to get her book she heard Ms. Whipple say loudly and angrily, "Lacy, what are you doing?"

Lacy's big grin vanished and her head jerked up as she attempted to move her phone without looking like she was doing anything. It didn't work.

"Bring it here," said Ms. Whipple.

"What?" asked Lacy.

"You know what. Your phone. I want it—now."

Lacy mumbled something under her breath and took her phone and put it on the teacher's desk. As she did, it dinged indicating a text message. Lacy reached for it, but Ms. Whipple snatched the phone away from her and put it upside down at the back of her desk.

Lacy made a face.

"My parents will be in to talk to you," the girl said with her hands on her hips.

"Yes, they will," replied Ms. Whipple. "And you will be in detention tonight, young lady."

As Lacy stomped back to her desk, Zoey grimaced. Oh no, she thought, I'm going to be in detention with her.

And everything got worse.

Chapter Three

Fight!

Lunch time was a disaster for Zoey. She was planning to stay in the room, but Ethan, the shyest boy in the class, asked her to go with him. She knew he felt sorry for her.

Stares came from everywhere as the two walked into the cafeteria and filled their trays. Smart-butt Dacoda who always made wisecracks about her was behind her in line and she heard him say, "There she is, right ahead of us. Zoey Zimmer, the one who ruined my experiment. I left it in the lab and there's nothing left of it."

Ethan turned around and said, "You know she didn't do it on purpose. And why is everything always about you?"

Dacoda immediately left the line and walked up to Ethan. Zoey put her hand on Ethan's shoulder. She knew how mean Dacoda could be.

"Come on Ethan, ignore him. He's not bothering me. Let's go sit down."

As they started to walk off, Dacoda grabbed Ethan by the arm.

"Don't you ever talk to me that way, you little punk. We don't want your kind around here. You and your ... mother need to go back where you came from."

Ethan's eyes narrowed. He slowly took his drink from his tray and poured it all over the front of Dacoda's pants. Dacoda knocked the tray out of Ethan's hand and grabbed him and the two wrestled to the floor rolling in the milk, the peas, and the pie.

"Fight!" yelled several people and the teachers rushed to break it up.

Zoey sighed. Detention was going be interesting tonight.

Chapter Four

Detention

When the rest of her class jumped up at the final bell, Zoey sat sulking at her desk.

"Let's go, Zoey," said Ms. Whipple. "Coach Mitchell is waiting."

Zoey groaned. Could her day get any worse? Of all the teachers to get for detention, he was the absolute awfullest. And the coach would tell all his stories about how great he was in baseball, but he only played in the minor leagues. Now she'd have to spend her evening with three egotistical goof-heads. Only Ethan was worth being near and he was so shy around girls she could hardly get him to talk.

Zoey dragged herself out of her seat and followed Ms. Whipple and the others to the detention room. The coach was waiting and started into his usual story. Zoey heard the first sentences where he made a triple play from shortstop and saved the game.

The rest sounded like blah, blah, blah as she stared out the window with her hands on her cheeks.

Wait! She sat up straight. What were those people doing? Across the back field, close to the old graveyard, a group of strange looking people walked toward the school. Actually, they didn't walk. More like staggered. That's weird, thought Zoey. Why are they all walking so funny and so slow?

Coach Mitchell had started on one of his other baseball stories as Zoey stood up to get a better view.

"Sit down, Zoey," said the coach. "You're not supposed to be wandering around."

Zoey ignored him and squinted at the people.

"Sit down," he said louder.

Zoey screamed.

Chapter Five

Zombies Everywhere

"It's zombies!" Zoey shouted. "They're coming toward the school."

"Don't be ridiculous," said Coach Mitchell.

Everybody crowded together at the windows.

"Sure look like zombies," said Lacy.

"No," said the Coach. "It's just people dressed up like zombies."

"Why," asked Dacoda.

"How would I know?" asked the Coach.

"Go find out," said Zoey.

"Me?"

"Yeah," said Zoey. "You're the teacher, the adult."

"And the super athlete," said Lacy, rolling her eyes.

Coach Mitchell stared out the window, then looked at the four students. He swallowed and left the classroom.The four had their faces pressed against the glass as the Coach eased out the back door.

“They see him,” said Dacoda. “And they’re going after him.”

They watched as the Coach cautiously approached the creatures waving his arms and saying something to them.

“He’s running,” shouted Lacy.

The coach tried to get back into the school, but the way was blocked by zombies. He ran toward the back field, but was quickly surrounded.

“OMG!” screamed Lacy. “They’re biting him.”

“They really are zombies,” whispered Zoey.

“But they’re not eating his brains,” said Dacoda. “I thought that’s what zombies do.”

“Duh,” said Lacy. “It’s the Coach. Why would they waste their time.”

“Look,” said Zoey. “The Coach has turned into a zombie. Ugh. He looks awful.”

“A definite improvement,” said Lacy.

“Let’s get outta here,” said Dacoda.

They rushed to the classroom door to find zombies in the hallway. They slammed the door and piled desks against it.

Ethan slumped into a chair. "You know, this is scientifically impossible. Dead people don't come back to life. That graveyard is over one hundred years old. There are no bodies left—just dust."

"Hey," said Dacoda. "The nerd taco-eater finally speaks to tell us what our eyes don't really see."

Ethan jumped up. "Call me that again and you'll be missing teeth."

"Si, little señor. I'm trembling in my boots."

Ethan started after Dacoda, and Zoey grabbed him. Lacy held Dacoda.

"Shut up, Dacoda," said Lacy. "You're stupid. Why don't you go out there with the zombies. Your brain would be safe."

"Oh, the rich little cheerleader who has her butler do her homework is calling me stupid."

"Knock it off," said Zoey. "We're in trouble here and we have to work together."

They watched as other teachers rushed out trying to stop the zombies.

"Look," said Zoey. "Mrs. Sanchez is fighting them with a chair."

"Mamá!" cried Ethan. "I gotta go help her."

He started toward the door and the others held him back. They watched as Mrs. Sanchez turned into a zombie.

"Zoey," said Ethan. He had tears running down his cheeks. "You can fix this. Your formula must have caused this somehow, so you can figure out how to reverse it."

Zoey shook her head. "I have no idea what I did. How could my experiment cause zombies?"

"But you know how you made the formula, right?"

"I think so. I made some notes."

"Then you can reverse what happened."

The pain on Ethan's face made Zoey's heart hurt, but she couldn't do this. Rather than depending on her, they'd be better off making a run for it.

"Please, Zoey," said Ethan. "At least try."

"Yeah, Zoey," said Lacy, "you're our only hope."

Zoey stared out at the zombies and the teachers trying to fight them. Strange, they weren't eating the teacher's brains.

Just turning them into zombies.

She had to do something.

“Okay, I’ll try, but we have to get to the lab and we’re trapped in here.”

Chapter Six

The Football Play

"I'm a football player," said Dacoda.

Lacy sighed, a big loud sigh.

Dacoda clenched his teeth. "As I was saying before I was rudely interrupted, I'm a football player. I know how to run through people that are trying to catch me. We can do it. Just follow me."

Lacy snickered. "It seems to me that you were tackled on every play in the last game."

"So, a blocker wasn't doing his job."

"It's always somebody else with you, isn't it? It's never your fault. You always do it right."

"What do you know? And besides do you have a better idea?"

Nobody said anything.

"Let's try it," said Ethan. "Tell us what to do, Dacoda."

Dacoda's eyes widened and he smiled.

"All right, little buddy, we can do this."

Dacoda went to the whiteboard and mapped out a play. He would go out first and try to draw the zombies away while the others made a mad dash for the lab. Lacy was skeptical and sure it wouldn't work, but she agreed to try it with the others.

They cracked the door open. The hallway was empty.

"Let's go," whispered Dacoda. They eased out the door and crept down the hallway. A zombie appeared at the far end of the hallway behind them and growled. Other zombies showed up both in front and behind them.

Dacoda hollered, "Come and get me," as he ducked down a side corridor.

The others waited until the zombies followed Dacoda and started running for the lab.

Dacoda made a loop through the hallways and was coming back when the three made it to the lab just as two zombies neared them. The zombies shuffled into the corridor between Dacoda and the others. He was trapped.

"They've got him cornered," said Ethan.

"We've got to help him," said Lacy. "You stay here, Zoey, you're the only one that can do the formula and we'll go try to help Dacoda."

"No way. I'm going with you, but we need some weapons."

Ethan pointed to a nearby cleaning closet and yanked open the door. Mops, brooms and buckets lined the wall.

"Probably the best we're gonna get," he said.

The three grabbed some of each and ran up behind the two zombies heading towards Dacoda.

Zoey hit one over the head with a mop handle. The creature growled and turned. It looked like her music teacher, Mr. Klein.

"Sorry, Mr. Klein," she said as she smacked his head with a bucket. The zombie staggered back and fell against the wall.

Lacy and Ethan used brooms and mops to pin the other zombie against the wall.

"Run, Dacoda," they shouted

Dacoda sprinted, leaping over the zombie crouched on the floor.

He shouted, "Touchdown."

The others threw down their mops and ran with him. A zombie was coming down the corridor to the right and Zoey veered toward it and kicked it in the stomach. She ran back as other zombies came from the other direction and the four piled into the lab, slamming the door behind them.

They pushed tables and chairs up against it and they collapsed on the floor.

"Whoa," said Zoey. "That was close. Are you okay, Dacoda?"

"I'm fine. One of the zombies grabbed me, but I was able to get away before it bit me. So I think I'm okay."

Lacy grinned at him. "Well if you turn into a zombie, we'll just have to kill you."

He laughed. "Fair enough."

"You know," said Zoey, "the zombies are not eating the teachers' brains."

"Yikes," said Lacy. "That means they're after ours. Young brains. And we're the only kids in school."

"Well, they're not going to get them," said Dacoda.

"Yeah," they all said as they pumped their fists in the air.

Zoey grinned at the other three. "You know what has happened? We've become a team."

Chapter Seven

The Missing Formula

"The Z-team," said Dacoda.

"And we're gonna kick some zombie butt," said Lacy.

"Yeah," said Ethan, "and now Zoey can come up with a way to change everybody back, including my Mom."

"I really don't know where to start."

"You can figure it out," said Ethan. "We know you can."

"That's right," said Dacoda. "We're counting on you, Zoe. You're our chemistry genius. And start with your notes."

"I'm not a genius. Remember I made this mess."

"Actually, it isn't as bad as it looks. It was mostly smoke. Let's straighten things up so you have a place to work."

Zoey took a deep breath. She could do this.

"Here's your space," said Lacy. "Nice and clean, and we found chemicals in a cabinet that weren't damaged. We brought them out for you."

Zoey nodded. Her throat was tight.

She cleaned her smoke-smudged safety glasses and put on her lab coat. Zoey dug out her notes stored in a drawer with the chemicals she had brought from home. She gasped. One of the chemicals had spilled on the notes blurring her writing. She couldn't quite make out what chemicals she used originally. She'd have to guess.

Zoey found an unbroken beaker and with shaky hands began to add chemicals from her notes and trying to figure out the blurred chemicals.

The mixture began to smoke. She didn't remember it doing that before. Something was wrong and she suspected the problem was the last chemical she had added. It was smeared from the spill, but she could tell it was two words. But which words? It looked like baking soda so she had added that.

Her stomach felt like it was full of angry bees.

"Okay," she said trying to sound more optimistic than she was.

"Let's try it."

Two zombies were milling around outside the window. She opened the window and hollered to them.

"Here, zombie. Come here little, gross zombie."

One lumbered towards her mumbling, "Brains."

When it was close enough, Zoey threw the mixture on the zombie. It screamed and stopped. The creature looked confused for a moment and then looked at her again. She quickly closed the window as the zombie lumbered up to it and began beating on it. The other one approached and also pounded on the window. Lacy closed the shades.

Zoey slumped to the floor with her head in her hands.

"It didn't work. I don't have any idea of what I'm doing. We're doomed."

Chapter Eight

The Secret Ingredient

Ethan got down beside her. "Don't give up. This was just your first try. Try again, there's no rush."

The banging on the windows got louder and now there were zombies pounding on the door, too.

"Uh, maybe you could rush just a little," said Lacy.

Zoey pushed herself up from the floor.

"I've got it all figured out except for one chemical that has two words. My notes are smeared and I can't read the words. See what you think."

They all crowded around the smeared paper and made guesses.

"Calcium carbonate," said Lacy.

"Boric acid," said Ethan.

"Sodium bicarbonate," said Dacoda.

"No," said Zoey. "Not any to those. I tried the baking soda. There was something else, but I can't remember what."

The pounding on the glass got louder.

Lacy went to a window and peeked out behind the shades. She gulped.

"We're in big trouble," she said. "The zombies are using rocks to beat on the window."

"I remember," screamed Zoey. "Acetic acid. Find it, quick."

She dumped out the first solution and added everything else back as before, except for the baking soda. The solution didn't smoke.

"Hurry," she said, as the pounding intensified.

"Oh no," said Ethan. He held up a plastic jug that said acetic acid. The top was missing and the jug was empty.

"Now we really are doomed," said Lacy.

"No," said Zoey. "When I got a bucket out of the cleaning closet I saw a bottle of vinegar behind it."

They all jumped up.

"But how are we going to get to the closet?" asked Lacy.

"Lab tables," said Ethan.

"Huh?" asked Dacoda.

"Yeah," said Ethan. "We'll turn the tables on their sides to make like a wall. They're heavy and the zombies are walking slow and stiff. They won't get over the tables."

"Might work," said Dacoda and he fist-bumped Ethan. "We'll have to quickly open the door and slide a table out to block the zombies."

"We'll need two," said Lacy. "One to block each side of the hall."

"Right," said Zoey. "And we'll need something to divert them until we get the tables out."

Lacy picked up a science book. "This'll do it. These things are heavy enough to crack your spine carrying them in a backpack, so I bet they'll slow down a zombie."

"And I'll do the throwing," said Dacoda. "I'm good at that."

Lacy grabbed the edge of the science book and heaved it at the classroom door. It smacked into the door with a loud crash.

They heard the zombies scrambling to get back from the door.

"Ooookay," said Dacoda. "We can throw the books and Zoey and Ethan can push the tables."

Together they turned over the tables and lined them up. Only one would go through the door at a time so the book throwers had to keep the zombies away until the first table was out.

They beat on the door to chase the zombies back and Dacoda yanked it open.

Ethan got on his hands and knees and pushed a table as Dacoda and Lacy threw books. As soon as he was out the door, Zoey pushed her table and the other two followed with Dacoda still throwing books and Lacy bringing the formula.

They pushed the table down the hallway forcing the zombies back until they got to the cleaning closet. They all squeezed in and slammed the door.

Chapter Nine

"It Didn't Work!"

Lacy set the solution on the floor. Zoey grabbed a bottle of vinegar and poured some into the solution. She stirred with her pencil and added some to a spray bottle she found.

She looked at the others. "Ready?"

They all nodded. Dacoda cracked open the door and a zombie immediately tried to force its way in. Zoey sprayed the creature. Nothing happened.

"Close the door!" she hollered.

Dacoda and Lacy grabbed the door handle, but the zombie had already gotten part of its arm into the room.

They forced the door closed and the zombie's severed hand fell to the floor. The hand inched its way across the linoleum.

"Eew," said Lacy as they backed away.

"It didn't work," said Zoey, dropping her head..

Ethan climbed a ladder stored in the back of the closet. He pushed open a ceiling tile and crawled into the ceiling.

"What are you doing?" asked Dacoda. "Get back down here."

"No, we're all gonna turn into zombies anyway. I want to be with my mother. I'll crawl to her classroom. I saw her going in there."

And Ethan disappeared.

"Look," shouted Lacy.

She pointed towards the zombie hand. It was now dust.

"Did it really work?" asked Zoey.

"It did," said Dacoda. "It just took a while. We'll have to spray and run. Fill up more bottles."

"What about the teachers?" asked Lacy. "Will they become dust?"

The three looked at each other.

"No," said Zoey. "The graveyard zombies were dust to start with. The teacher zombies will go back to humans ... I hope."

"You're right," said Ethan. "Let's go."

They filled up three bottles and cracked the door again spraying in all directions. They shut the door and waited a few minutes then peered out to see small piles of dust. They dashed out spraying as they went and dodging zombies.

"Where are the teachers?" hollered Lacy.

"Looks like they're in their classrooms," yelled Zoey. "Where else would a dead teacher go? Let's get the real zombies first, and then save the teachers."

Chapter Ten

Life to a Dead School

The three split up, spraying as they ran. They found the zombie teachers sitting in their classrooms at their desks heedlessly moving piles of papers from one side of the desk to the other.

Zoey's first destination was Ethan's mother's classroom.

She got there in time to see Ethan crash through the ceiling and land on the floor in front of the zombie that was his mother. The creature stood up and started toward him with its mouth open.

"It's me, Mom," said Ethan.

"Brains," mumbled the zombie.

Ethan backed up. "Mom, it's me, Ethan."

The zombie was forcing him into a corner when Zoey rushed up with the spray bottle. She sprayed the zombie and it changed into Ethan's mother. The woman collapsed into a chair.

"I feel exhausted," she said.

"Ethan, what are you doing in that corner and what happened to the ceiling? Did you do that?"

Ethan's mom doesn't remember anything, thought Zoey. Zoey shook her head at Ethan.

He caught on. "Yeah, I did. I was climbing through the duct to ... uh, see where it went and fell through."

"You've never done anything like this before. Detention and now this. I'm really disappointed in you. And you know you will lose your privileges for a month. Now get back to your room."

"I'm sorry, Mom, and I really don't mind if it's two months."

He ran to his mother and grabbed her in a big hug and held on until she peeled him off, pointing to the door. As he zoomed past Zoey, he stopped long enough to give her a quick kiss on the cheek and he whispered to her, "I'll go straighten up the lab and the hall."

Ethan's mother's mouth hung open.

Dacoda, Lacy, and the Coach came into the room.

"Are you okay, Mrs. Sanchez?" asked Dacoda and he gave her a quick hug.

Her eyes widened. "Of course, why do you ask?"

Zoey standing behind Mrs. Sanchez held a finger to her lips. The other two nodded.

"Um," said Lacy. "We heard a crash and came to check on you."

"Check on me? Nobody has ever done that before."

"I'm sorry for all the stupid stuff I've said," stated Dacoda. "I'm really glad you and Ethan are here."

"Come on kids," said Coach. "Back to the detention room."

"Okay, Coach," said Lacy grinning and the three left.

"What is going on, Zoey?" asked Mrs. Sanchez. "Everybody is acting different. Better. It's almost like your experiment causing the lab to blow up brought life to a dead school."

"You have no idea, Mrs. Sanchez," said Zoey. "You have no idea."

The Secret of the Cavern

One

The Journal

"The page is missing."

"I can see that, doofus, but why?"

Josh closed the journal and handed it to his sister. "You know everything, so you tell me."

Kris rolled her eyes at her younger brother. "Well, you're the one that *feels* things. So what do you think?"

"It has something to do with our grandfather."

"Brilliant, Sherlock. We're standing in his old house and you found that in a musty closet."

Josh sighed. "Can we ever have just a normal conversation?"

"You started it, but forget that. What are we going to do with this journal?"

"Even without the missing map, there's decent instructions to get to a hidden cave," said Josh. "Let's follow them. There has to be something special there or why would it be in the journal.

"We already know about the cliff that's mentioned. Should we tell mom and dad?"

The two stared at each other.

"Sorry, dumb question."

"They'll spend the day arguing," said Kris. "They'll never miss us."

The two grabbed their backpacks and worked their way out of the fallen-down old house on the rear of their property. A house that had been built by their great grandfather and lived in by their grandfather and grandmother. Their parents had built a new house closer to the road on the same property.

They helped one another climb over the fence between their property and the national forest. They weren't supposed to be out in this wilderness by themselves, but they went into the area quite often. Their parents never found out.

"Did you bring your bear spray?" asked Josh.

"No, nobody's seen a bear around here in years. Why should I?

Josh shrugged and opened the journal.

"This says he traveled west for about an hour until he got to the white faced cliffs. We've been that far. But I'm not sure about the rest of it and I sure wish I knew who wrote this."

"Looking at the age of the book and the writing, it has to be great grandfather."

"Probably. Let's go."

The warm morning sun reached the treetops and they removed their jackets and tied them to the backpacks. They got to the cliffs before nine.

"Now what?" asked Josh.

"What does it say?"

"Not much. It says to turn east and follow the ridge line and then see the map. I wish we had the map."

"Well, we don't," snarled Kris. "And since you think this is so important, we have to figure it out without the map."

"I don't know why it's important, but it is."

Kris shook her head in disgust and moved away from the cliff towards the ridge line.

"Let's go, I don't want to waste my whole day out here."

She led with long strides until they left the tree cover and entered a rocky outcrop. They struggled through loose gravel and climbed over rocks and boulders. Sweating and gasping, they took a break and pulled out their water bottles. As Josh took a swig, he suddenly jerked.

"What's the matter?" asked Kris.

"Something is watching us."

Kris twisted her neck. "There's nothing here."

"There is, but I can't see it either. I know it's here."

Kris opened her mouth to speak when she suddenly pointed.

"Over there," she whispered. "I saw movement."

They both climbed down behind the boulder away from the movement. And waited.

Josh grabbed Kris's arm as the face of a mountain lion appeared in a gap between two boulders.

"It's a lion," he said. "There's not supposed to be mountain lions in this part of the country," said Kris.

"You tell him that. I'm getting out of here."

"We can't run. It's a lot faster than we are."

"I'm not going to stay here and get eaten. Why don't you wait for it to come down here and when it eats you, I'll have more time to get away."

Josh stood up and started running.

"Wait," hollered Kris. And she ran after him.

Josh ran toward the woods and Kris's long legs allowed her to catch up with him.

"Why are you going this way? The trees will give it more places to hide from us."

"I'm looking for a tree to climb."

"Dumb bunny," panted Kris. "It's a cat. They can climb trees."

Josh glanced back. "I can see it. It's following us."

"If it attacks, we have to fight. We'll use sticks and rocks. Maybe we can chase it off."

"Okay," huffed Josh. "But keep on running, maybe he'll give up."

Up ahead the ground dipped and the weeds and grasses were taller. The two didn't hesitate and charged headlong into the marsh. Their feet touched nothing as they dropped, screaming, into an abyss.

Two

In The Cavern

They fell for what seemed like forever and splashed into a pool of water that felt as hard as ice. Gasping for breath, they struggled to the side.

"Are you okay?" asked Kris.

"I think so. That was a long way down. I thought I landed on rock."

"It felt like it. Have you got your backpack?"

"Yeah, but everything is soaked, including my flash-light. It's dark down here."

"And there's no way up," said Kris. "Look, it's like a dome. Impossible to climb."

"I don't see any other light. Do you think there's a way out?"

"How would I know? And we wouldn't be in this mess if you hadn't started running."

"And what were you going to do? At least we're still alive. The mountain lion didn't get us."

"We're alive, for now ..."

Neither said a word. They listened to the plop, plop of water dripping through the dome opening. Their eyes stared into the darkness.

"I've got my emergency flashlight," said Josh. "It's sealed."

He rummaged around in his pack.

"It's so small," said Kris. "Let's take our regular flash-lights out and take them apart to dry."

They carried their packs over to a flat rock where they could get enough light from the dome and emptied out the contents. They found their flashlights and took them apart.

"Let's wait a while," said Kris, "and let them dry completely."

"I can't wait," said Josh.

He picked up his flashlight and blew into it and waved it through the air.

After a few minutes he put it back together and pushed the switch.

The light flashed to life.

"Use your big one," said Kris, "and I'll use the emergency one. We'll have enough light and it will save my batteries."

The two repacked their backpacks and started into the gloom.

They trudged for an hour following the water, knowing that they could always find their way back to the dome. After climbing over rocks and boulders and splashing through the water, they stopped to take a break.

As Josh sat down, he dropped his flashlight. It went out. He picked it up and shook it, but it didn't come on.

"Can't you do anything right?" asked Kris.

Josh grunted and took his flashlight apart. As Kris shined her light on it, Josh stopped, and stared at the darkness.

"What?"

"Turn off your light, Kris. I think I see something."

Kris switched off the light and the two stared into the gloom ahead.

"You're right," exclaimed Kris. "I see it too. It's a dot of light in the distance."

Three

Grandfather

"You think that's a way out?"

Kris sighed. "I don't know. Why do you always ask me these crazy questions?"

"Well, you act like you know everything. That's why mom and dad are getting a divorce. Because you always are the number one know-it-all."

"You shut up. It's not me, it's you. You're the weird one. Feeling things that nobody else can. It's creepy."

"I wish we didn't always fight," said Josh. "And I wish mom and dad weren't getting a divorce."

"Wishing won't solve anything. Come on, let's find a way out of here."

Kris put the batteries back into her flashlight, but it didn't work. The two crept through the inky blackness using Josh's emergency flashlight heading towards a pinpoint of light that could be their escape.

"Stop," said Josh.

"What's the matter?"

"There's somebody there."

"Don't be stupid."

"Hello," shouted Josh.

"Be quiet. There is nobody here but us, you ..."

"Hello," echoed back to them from the cavern.

"I told you."

Josh jumped up and started running toward the sound.

"Wait. What if it's a criminal, or worse?"

"It's not," Josh hollered back at her. "I think I know who it is."

They followed the water in the direction of the light and the sound.

Soon they saw that the light was not an exit, but a large, oval-shaped device glowing in the darkness.

And in front of it was a shadow of a tall man waiting for them.

"Wait," whispered Kris. "We don't know what this is. Let's be careful."

"I know what it is."

Josh walked up to the figure that they now saw was a man.

An old man.

"Hello," said Josh. "Who are you and why are you down here? And what's that thing?"

"Kids," said the man. "Kids. I thought it was somebody who had come to rescue me."

"No," said Kris. "We fell in a hole and we don't know how to get out."

"The same as me. I'm sorry to tell you, but there's no way out."

The two looked at each other in fear.

"No way out," mumbled Josh.

"Don't give up yet," said Kris. "I might be able to find an exit."

Josh snorted. He stared at the man. "I think I know who you are. What's your name?"

"How could you possibly know me?" the man replied. "But my name is Fred Williams."

Kris gasped and Josh grabbed the man's arm.

"You're our grandfather," he said.

The man's mouth fell open. "Your grandfather, how could that be?"

"Mother has told us how you disappeared years ago," said Kris. "Nobody knew where you went. Our mother's name is Alice."

"What year is this?" asked the man, his hands shaking.

"2019," said Kris.

The man fell to his knees. "I've been down here thirty years and the first people I see are my grandchildren.

"But my wife, your grandmother ..."

The children shook their heads. She had died years before.

The man's bony arms reached out and pulled them to him. His sobs shook his body and the two children held him until he was able to speak. "Now you will die here with me."

Four

Inside The Craft

"No," the two said in unison.

"We'll figure a way out," said Kris.

"What is that thing behind you?" asked Josh.

"I really don't know. I guess some kind of space craft, but I've been unable to get into it. There's no way to open it, but there must be something inside. I've tried for years. But it's what has kept me alive. Come and see my farm."

He led them around the glowing device to a flat area where plants and trees grew. The two stood stunned to see apple trees, pear trees, and vegetables growing in a cave deep in the earth.

"This thing, whatever it is, provides heat and light for the plants to grow.

"I guess seeds fall through the opening in the dome and wash up here and sprout. The apple trees came from an apple.

"One I found floating in the water and I took its seeds and planted them. The creek is full of fish, too. Drawn by the heat and light.

"So I have plenty to eat, and I'm warm, but I can't go too far from this warmth. I found flint in the cave and with my pocket knife, I can build a fire.

"I regularly take torches and explore, but I would die if I couldn't get back here. I always thought someone would find me. There is another entrance because my father found it and wrote about it in his journal, but he never found this thing."

He pointed to the glowing machine.

Josh reached in his backpack and pulled out the journal.

The grandfather took it and lightly caressed it. He walked to the small hut he had built with stones and wood and came back with a missing page. It was tattered, but still readable. Josh took it and fitted it into the journal. "Maybe the three of us can figure a way out," he said.

The old man shook his head and sat on a rock.

"I can't imagine how."

Josh turned to the craft and ran his hands over the smooth surface.

"It's here to tell us something," he said.

"Don't pay any attention to him, Grandfather," said Kris. "He has these weird feelings."

"I thought Grandfather was down here," said Josh. "And I was right. She's a smart aleck who thinks she's always right and she's the reason our parents are getting a divorce."

"Don't you dare say that again. I'm not the reason, you are. We are all tired of you and your goofy feelings."

"Hold on," said the grandfather. "I doubt either one of you is the reason for the divorce. It's not your fault, it's your parents' fault. And who did your mother marry anyway?"

"His name is Tom," said Kris. "Mom said he lived down the street when she was a little girl."

"I remember him" said grandfather.

"He was always around the house. I often had to run him home."

The man put his arm around the two children. "It appears to me that you two complement one another."

"She's never given me a compliment in my whole life," said Josh.

"What I meant," said the man, "is that you both have a special talent and, for the first time, I think maybe we really can get out of here. If you can learn to work together."

They looked at each other and barely nodded.

"Let's look at this thing," said Josh. "I know, I mean ... I feel, that it has a message for us. But we have to figure out how to get inside. And what keeps it glowing?"

"Obviously, it's nuclear powered," said Kris.

The three walked around the craft and on the backside Josh pointed and hollered. "A touchscreen."

"A what?" asked the grandfather.

"A touchscreen," said Kris. "It's a way to input information into a computer or device."

"I thought it was a window, so I beat on it with a rock. Didn't even scratch it."

Josh went to it and touched it with his finger.

Nothing happened. Kris pushed him aside and put her hand flat against the smooth surface. She held it there for a few seconds and a screen popped up.

The grandfather ran to it. "What is that?"

"It recognized my hand and brought up a new screen. But now it's showing a place for a password."

She glanced at her brother. "Do you feel anything?"

"No, but it has to be something humans would know."

Kris nodded and jerked back towards the touch-screen. "I got it."

She drew with her finger in the space for the password the symbol E=MC2.

"Einstein's theory," whispered grandfather.

Kris punched a square box hoping that it was the enter key.

A rumbling came from deep inside the craft. The glow changed from a bright white to a reddish color and they heard a sound on the other side of the device.

They hurried around and found.

A door opening.

The three paused at the entrance. A pale green light filled the circular room and opposite them was an array of screens of different sizes.

One was flashing red.

"This is amazing," said Kris.

Their grandfather held onto the side of the device seemingly unable to move.

"Yes, yes," he said. "I never dreamed all this was inside. But what does it mean?"

Josh was already sitting in a chair before the flashing screen, his hands poised to touch the screen.

"Don't touch anything, Goof Head," said Kris.

Her grandfather shook his head at her.

"I mean, please, Josh, don't touch anything until I can look at it. You might launch us into space."

Josh reluctantly got up from the chair, but his eyes were locked on the screen. The screen with red colors intertwining and flashing.

"It's waiting for us to do something," he said. "And it's going to tell us something important."

Kris opened her mouth to speak, but caught her

grandfather's eyes and closed her mouth. She went and sat in the chair before the screen. She put her hand up as before and the screen reacted. The red vanished and in its place was a three-dimensional view of what appeared to be planets in space.

They were all moving in arcs around a sun.

"It looks like our solar system," said grandfather.

"It is," shouted Josh.

Then they all gasped as another celestial body came moving through the solar system. It was glowing red with a long tail and came from behind the sun. It moved past the first two planets and smashed into the third causing it to fly apart in a huge explosion.

"The earth," cried Kris. "It hit the earth."

Five

A Way Out

They knew, they all knew, what the spacecraft had come to tell them. The earth was in danger and would be hit by a huge meteor.

"We have to get out of here," whispered Josh. "We've got to tell someone. Maybe they can stop it with an A-bomb."

"But when will this happen?" asked grandfather.

"I'm sure," said Kris, "that an astronomer would know exactly when the planets are aligned the way they are on the screen. That would give them the exact date."

Then her hand moved toward what looked like an arrow on the right side of the screen. She tapped it and the screen changed again.

This time they saw an interactive map of a large body of water surrounded by land and on one end was a narrow opening. At the opening was a huge mountain of stone. Around the water were cities and traveling between the cities were old-fashioned boats. Ones using sails. And on an island at the end of a long narrow peninsula of land was a mountain spewing smoke.

"What is this?" asked Josh.

Kris rubbed her chin. "It's the Mediterranean. See, there's Gibraltar, and there's Italy."

Her finger traced the way around the sea pointing to other recognizable landmarks. Egypt and the Nile River were visible, as well as the pyramids. As they watched, the smoke from the volcano intensified and fire began coming out of its opening. Then it exploded raining fire and ash down on a town at its base.

Kris jumped up. "The volcano, it's Mount Vesuvius," she shouted.

"And it's destroying Pompeii," said grandfather.

The screen went blank and a number appeared. 1,948.

Kris slumped in her chair. She put her hands over her face. "That's how many years since the eruption of Mount Vesuvius that the meteor will hit."

"I don't understand," said Josh.

"What the aliens have done," said Kris, "is show us an event that everyone would know because of its historical significance. And then they told us how long after that the meteor would hit. But I don't know the year it erupted."

"I do," said grandfather. "I had to write a paper about Pompeii when I was in high school. I've never forgotten the date. It was 79 A.D."

"It's C.E., now, grandfather," said Josh.

"Forget that," grumbled Kris. "Let me figure a date."

She opened her pack to find her phone, when Josh said, "2027."

"I forgot you can do math in your head. Kind of weird."

"It's a wonderful gift," said grandfather patting Josh's arm.

"That's not long at all" said Kris. "There's only few years before it smashes the earth. What can the world do?"

Josh sat down at another screen and put his hand on it.

"What are you doing?" asked Kris as she jumped up and ran to him.

"It has a map."

"What do you mean?"

"It will show us a map, it has to. That's the only way out and we have to get out to tell people."

Kris scrunched down beside him and the two of them touched and scrolled the screen. It was a screen of maps. Maps of space, of the earth from above, and then one of the area surrounding their house. They could see their town, their school and almost make out their house.

"Zoom in," said Kris.

Josh looked at her.

"Pinch like you do on your iPad."

Josh pinched the screen until they saw the white cliffs and the ridge line and he moved the screen directly over the hole they fell through.

"Now what?" asked Kris.

Josh kept pinching until the hole became a blur and then the screen showed the inside of the cavern.

Kris screamed and the grandfather gasped.

"You did it, Josh," said Kris. "We can see the whole cave."

The grandfather pointed to the screen. "And there's the exit. It shows the sun shining through it. We'll be able to get out."

He slumped into the other chair and buried his face in his hands. The children rushed to him and put their arms around him.

Then Kris stood up. "We got the map, but we'll have to find something to write it on to take it with us. Look around and see what's here."

There were a few cabinets and drawers, but only one held anything. The grandfather held it up.

"That looks like a mouse," said Josh.

"It doesn't look anything like a mouse," said grandfather. "It doesn't have a tail or ears or feet."

"A computer mouse, grandfather. You wouldn't have ever seen one."

"Wait," said Kris. "I bet there's a way for us to download the map to my phone."

She opened her backpack and found the plastic bag she had her phone sealed in when she was hiking. She took it out and turned it on. An image of it immediately appeared on the alien computer screen.

"Wow," said Josh. "Now what?"

Kris touched the map and moved her finger to the phone image. The map immediately popped up on the phone in her hand.

Six

No Way Across

"You did it," shouted Josh. And he hugged her. She grimaced, but let him hold her.

"You both work so well together," said the grandfather.

The two looked at each other in amazement.

"Let's go," said the grandfather. "Should I bring this mouse thing?"

"Yes," said Kris. "We can show it to the authorities to convince them about what we know."

Grandfather went into his shelter to gather his belongings.

"Do I need to bring my torches?" he asked.

"Oh, no," said Kris. "Our batteries. They won't last until we get out."

"And what about your phone?" asked Josh.

"It should be okay. I charged it before we left this morning, but our flashlights won't last."

"I'll bring my torches," said the grandfather. "I'm not waiting another thirty years."

He put his things in Josh's backpack.

They started into the coal-black darkness with a sputtering flashlight, a small LED, and a handful of sticks—with over five miles to go.

Kris led with her flashlight and phone, keeping her phone off to preserve the battery. They struggled through tight passages and over fallen rock and soon decided to rest.

Grandfather had packed apples and they each ate one.

"We need to shut off our lights while we're eating." said Kris.

She and Josh clicked off their flashlight. To their surprise, light filled the area.

"Your backpack, Josh," shouted Kris.

They opened it to find the mouse-like device from the space craft glowing brightly.

"I bet it is nuclear powered, too," said Kris.

"Yeah," said Josh.

"We'll get out now," said the grandfather with a broad grin.

They continued on until Kris's phone said it was 11:00 and they decided to sleep for a while. It had been a long day.

They found some soft dirt and stretched out. The grandfather told them more about finding the craft and how he discovered the way it got in the cave. He surmised it must have landed above the cavern and, during an earthquake, sunk below the ground. He had found tracks where it had slid through the mud to its present resting place.

The three finally fell asleep and slept for a few hours.

They awoke eager to continue the journey.

The map led them down passages the grandfather had never seen

They crawled through narrow openings and over sharp-edged rocks.

Often, what looked like a passage on the map, turned out to be a dead end.

They stopped to eat their last apple and power bar, and in the quiet, heard rushing water.

"It's a waterfall," said Josh.

"A waterfall," said the grandfather. "In father's journal he wrote about a waterfall. We must be nearly there."

He stood up, "Let's go, let's go. I want to see a real tree, not one of those spindly things I grew. And I want to see the sun. The glorious sun. And the blue sky."

He led at a fast pace with Kris giving him directions from her phone. The sound of falling water got louder until they climbed a slight rise and it appeared in front of them. The water was deep, fast, and, at least, twenty feet across and crashed down on fang-toothed rocks below. They looked at it in horror.

There was no way across.

Seven

Into The Sunshine

Josh grabbed his grandfather and the two held each other.

"My father wrote in the journal that he stopped at a waterfall and couldn't go any further. But he could see a glowing light in the distance.

"See. There it is. A pinpoint of light. The space ship. If we could have followed the stream, we'd been here sooner, but there was no way through.

"My father knew the light wasn't natural and that's why he wrote about it. And that's why I wanted to find the cave."

Kris put her hands on both of their shoulders. "We're not going to give up yet," she said.

"You're right," said their grandfather. "The three of us, together, can figure this out."

Josh and Kris together touched the mouse device.

"Sorry, Kris, but I feel something about this thing."

"I was just wondering myself what its purpose is."

"Do you think it can help us get out of here?" asked the grandfather.

"It's all we have," replied Kris.

She held it in her hand and ran her fingers over it. She poked at it in several places. And then she handed it to Josh.

His eyes widened and he grinned at her. He took the device and held it against his cheek caressing it lightly. "It needs a number," he said.

"What do you mean?" asked Kris.

"We need to input a number. I'm not sure how."

Kris took it back from him and turned it over and over. "There are no seams or cracks. Nothing appears to open."

She stared at it some more and then yelled, "I've got it. The device is a touchscreen. What we need to do is just write the number on it with our finger."

"But what number," asked the grandfather.

"Again," she said, "it has to be something that everyone would know."

"Well," said the grandfather. "The first thing I would think of, would be pi."

Kris and Josh's eyes met. "Perfect," she said. "Josh, how many digits do you know of pi?"

"30 or so."

"Uh, maybe we won't need that many. Say them to me."

She wrote on the device with her finger as he called out the numbers. 3.141592 ...

The device flickered and began to glow brighter, then light shot out from the front of it.

"It's a laser," shouted Josh. He jerked his hand up and moved his finger toward the beam.

"Nooo!" hollered Kris.

She grabbed his hand and felt his finger.

"That was cra ..." She stopped, feeling her grandfather's eyes on her.

"Um, you shouldn't have done that. If it's a real laser, it would have cut your finger off.

"You've seen Star Wars. It's a good thing you didn't touch it."

"But I did. It felt like Gummi Bears."

Josh gently touched the beam again and then put his hand on it. Kris did the same. And Grandfather felt it.

"That's really weird," said Josh. He put both hands on it and pulled himself up on top of the beam. The device didn't move in Kris's hands. It easily held his weight.

"It spreads out," Josh said. "We can crawl across it."

He dropped to all fours and Kris shouted, "Josh, get off there, right now. We have to think about this first."

Reluctantly, he lowered himself back down. The grandfather reached out and touched the beam. "Lower it a bit," he said.

Kris held it at knee level and the grandfather crawled up on it.

"It will work, Kris. And I'll go across first in case something happens. It's best if an old man dies rather than a child."

Kris opened her mouth to say something, but her grandfather had already started.

"It feels really strange. Like crawling on some kind of goo, but it's holding me fine."

The man got to the other side and climbed off the beam.

"You're next, Josh." said Kris.

Josh climbed on the beam and made it across.

"What about you?" said the grandfather. "How are you going to get across?"

"I'll just wait here while you go get help."

"No," said Josh. "Set it on a rock. It will still work."

Kris set the device on a flat rock aiming it across the water. She put both hands on the beam and lifted her feet. It held her and the device didn't move.

"Okay, I'm coming."

She climbed on it and crawled across. Josh met her with a hug. She backed away from him.

They continued following the map for another mile until they saw the sun shining into the cavern.

"We made it," whispered the grandfather. He slowly walked toward the exit. Kris touched his arm. "Wait," she said. "You will probably need sunglasses."

"You're right," he said. "The sun will blind me."

Kris dug hers out of her backpack and the grandfather put them on. He continued to walk with a hesitating gait toward the bright sunshine. At last he stood in the rays and he laughed and danced around. Then he pulled himself out of the cavern and the two children followed.

The man stared at the sky in awe.

And then he marched directly to a large oak tree and put his arms around it and his face against the bark.

The second she exited the cavern, Kris pulled out the smart phone and dialed her parents. Her mom answered.

"Where are you and what have you been doing?" demanded her mother. "I tried to call you."

"It's a long story, Mom, but there's someone you need to see. Turn on FaceTime."

As the mother's face appeared, the grandfather walked up.

"Can I talk to her?" he asked.

Kris nodded.

"Alice," he said. "It's your father."

The mother gasped and her hand shook causing her face to move back and forth across the screen.

"It can't be," she sobbed. "Daddy, oh, Daddy. How is this possible?"

"We'll tell you all about it when we get back. I can't wait to see you. Call the authorities and have them there when we arrive. We'll explain some of it while we walk. And what's this about a divorce?"

Through her sobs the mother replied, "There isn't going to be any divorce. Tom and I were so worried about the children we decided that our differences are not nearly as important as the kids are. And we're going to work extra hard to be a real family again."

Josh jumped up and hollered and danced.

He threw his arms around Kris in a tackle-like hug. "I'm glad you're my sister, Kris."

Kris slowly put her arms around Josh and said, "And I'm glad that you're my brother, Josh."

The grandfather joined them, and said, "And I'm really, really glad that you're my grandchildren."

The Ghostly Math Teacher

1

Strange Eyes

The math teacher walked through the closed classroom door.

"Yikes," said Harry, and he leaned against the hallway wall. "Did you see that?"

"What?" asked Ginny.

"Mrs. Mills walked through that door."

"What do you mean, through the door? Nobody can do that."

"She did."

"Have you had your eyes checked lately?" asked Ginny.

"I see perfectly. I'm telling you, she walked through that door. She didn't open it. She just kinda melted through it."

"Harry, you better go see the nurse or the counselor."

"Listen, we both know something strange is going on at school. Mrs. Mills has been acting funny for a long time now and a bunch of the kids are, too. It's weird."

"Yeah. But you're just upset because you don't like math."

"I do like math, but she's asking the dumbest questions now. I have to study twice as hard to get them right."

"So, isn't that what our teachers are supposed to do? Make us work."

"Sure," said Harry. "But she's coming up with questions that have nothing to do with what we're studying. Even you said so. It's almost like she wants us to miss some of them."

They both looked up as one of the basketball stars walked toward them.

"Hello, Johnny," Harry said.

The tall boy didn't respond and stared straight ahead with a vacant look in his eyes.

"What's with him?" asked Ginny.

"He never acts stuck up."

"I don't think he's stuck up. I think it's something else. Something scary. This whole school has gotten really goofy. It's almost like it's haunted."

"Haunted? Like by ghosts? Oh, I get it. Ghosts can walk through doors, right?" She grinned at him.

"Don't be a smart aleck," he said. "I know what I saw."

Ginny grabbed his arm.

"Johnny disappeared."

"He must've gone into one of the classrooms," said Harry.

"No, those are the younger kids' classrooms and I didn't see a door open."

Harry smiled at Ginny, "Do you think he went through a door?"

"Absolutely not. But I think you're right that something really weird is going on in this school.

"We better get to math class now."

They rushed to the room and found their seats next to each other.

Ginny leaned over and whispered to Harry, "Mrs. Mills' eyes look just like Johnny's."

Harry nodded. "And some of the other kids have that look, too. Why?"

Ginny shrugged and opened her book.

"Another test today," announced Mrs. Mills. The class groaned.

She had an evil smile on her face as she passed out the papers.

"Good luck," she sneered.

Harry and Ginny exchanged glances. They had never seen her act this way before.

"Time," shouted Mrs. Mills. Only a short time had passed.

The class grumbled, complaining that it had hardly been fifteen minutes.

She gave them a few minutes more. And then took up the papers.

Harry whispered to Ginny, "How did you do?"

"I think I got them all. But number seven was especially tough. I was worried about it."

Harry agreed and started to say something else when Mrs. Mills suddenly stood up and said, "Several of you missed at least one question. I will need to see each of you one at a time to discuss this. The rest of you can work on your homework."

She called the name of the first and he stood and followed her out of the classroom.

"Why does she do that?" asked Harry. "She never did before. I first thought she was giving extra help to anybody who missed the question. But after she spends time with them, she doesn't seem to care if they ever miss a problem again?"

"That's not like her," said Ginny. "She's always been one of my favorite teachers. But not anymore. Something's changed."

The door opened and the boy and Mrs. Mills came back into the room. The student went to his seat behind Harry and Ginny.

They saw his eyes as he passed them. They both gasped. His eyes looked like Johnny's—and Mrs. Mills.

Ginny whispered to Harry,

"Meet me at the library in town after school."

Harry gave her a thumbs up.

2

Ghosts

The two friends walked together down the street after leaving the library.

"So what are you thinking?" asked Harry.

"I'm thinking that you may have been right about seeing Mrs. Mills walk through a door. I talked to some of the other kids before I came over here. I told them what you saw and …"

"Oh no," interrupted Harry. "Now I'm the laughingstock of the whole school."

"No, you aren't," said Ginny.

"Everybody is saying weird things are happening. And they all noticed that Johnny and some of the other students are not acting like themselves anymore. Just like Mrs. Mills."

"Why?"

"Nobody knows. But we have to find out. I think Mrs. Mills is doing something to the students to make them look like her."

"And what is she?" asked Harry, with a slight smile on his face.

Ginny looked down at her feet. "It makes no sense. But I think she's a ghost. All the ones that have that funny look in their eyes are acting like ghosts.

"Have you noticed that they never shake hands with anybody or talk to anybody anymore? They don't even do fist bumps."

"Yeah, now that you mention it. And you know what? When she takes those students out of the room to have her little talk with them, I bet she turns them into some kind of ghost or something freaky."

Ginny put her hand over her mouth. "I'm afraid you're right. But why?"

"Who knows? But whoever misses a problem will be a ghost."

They stopped and stared at each other.

"Oh, no," said Ginny.

"That means we can't miss a single question."

"I'm doomed.

"You're good at math because your mother is a physicist, but it's a struggle for me."

"I'm good because I study hard. You're good, too, but you need to spend more time on math and less on Minecraft. But we've gotta be better than good.

"We've got to be great. We'll study every day at lunch and do as much as we can in the evening. I'll help you. Mrs. Mills at least tells us what the test is going to be about."

Harry stuck his hands in his pockets. "It's hopeless. She'll get us eventually."

"Maybe, but we can buy enough time to figure this out. There has to be a reason."

"How do we fight a ghost?" asked Harry. "If some stranger came and tried to do something to us, I'd clobber him with my baseball bat.

"But it would go right through Mrs. Mills and she'd probably laugh at me."

Ginny's eyes widened and she grabbed Harry's arm.

"Harry, maybe the way you fight a ghost is to get another ghost to fight them."

"These math tests have fried your skull. What are you talking about?"

"Listen," exclaimed Ginny. "We can't hurt a ghost, right? But why couldn't another ghost do something?"

"Oh, great idea, Math Brain. So all we have to do is to find a ghost and convince it to fight Mrs. Mills."

"Don't be a jerk. We already have a ghost right here in Elkton."

Harry rubbed his chin. "You mean Pee Wee? That's what old man Jones is always telling people—that he sees Pee Wee, but Mr. Jones can't even find his way home."

"That's mean. And besides, other people have seen Pee Wee. At night, out on the ball field running the bases."

"Hmm," murmured Harry. "You might have something there. But how can we possibly find, and then talk to, somebody who's dead?"

"I don't know that answer," said Ginny and her

shoulders slumped.

"Let's think about it tonight," said Harry. "Maybe we'll come up with an idea. And tomorrow I want to try something. I'm going to try to touch Mrs. Mills."

3

The Plan

"Clear your desks for a test," said Mrs. Mills.

Four students groaned including Harry and Ginny. The rest stared straight ahead.

"Did you study?" whispered Ginny.

"Practically all night. I didn't touch Minecraft even once."

"No talking," said Mrs. Mills as she handed out the test.

When she placed the test on Harry's desk, he reached up to touch her hand. She jerked back and glared at him.

They turned over the sheet to find—decimals. An entire page of nothing but decimals.

"You have fifteen minutes," said Mrs. Mills.

Harry glanced at Ginny and nodded his head. He could do these.

Fifteen minutes later Mrs. Mills took up the papers and began to correct them. But she only looked at four and then stood up and pointed at a boy in the front row.

"You missed three of these," she sneered. "Come with me."

The other student had missed one problem and Mrs. Mills took her out of the room also. They both came back with the strange eyes.

The teacher scowled at Harry and Ginny. "You passed, both of you. But tomorrow we will have a geometry test."

Harry's mouth fell open. "But we haven't even studied geometry yet."

"No excuses. You have tonight to study."

Harry stumbled out of class and Ginny patted him on the back. "You can do it," she said.

"No, I can't. Geometry makes no sense and we haven't even had a class in it. I can't learn that tonight."

"I have an idea ..."

"Look," Harry interrupted.

They were standing in front of the display of Pee Wee's baseball bat. It was enclosed in a glass case.

"What?"

"I know how to get Pee Wee's ghost to help us."

Ginny raised her eyebrows.

"We'll take the bat to the ball field tonight and ask him to help. If there really is a ghost, he'll have to hold the bat again. And then Pee Wee can fight Mrs. Mills."

"Even if we contact him, how will he fight her?" asked Ginny.

"I don't know yet, but we'll figure that out. First I have to get the bat. Since I'm such a big fan of Pee Wee, the assistant principal gives me the key to the cabinet so I can polish up the bat. I'll go ask him if I can do that after school and then I'll take the bat home with me. I'll replace it tomorrow and nobody will miss it."

"Let's try it," said Ginny. "If it works you won't have to take the test tomorrow."

Harry hurried to the office.

He came back with a glum face.

"I can't do it tonight. He said that they'll be cleaning the hallway. I can do it tomorrow night, only by then I'll be a ghost. You'll have to get the bat, Ginny. Just tell the assistant principal that I had extra homework and you're going to polish it for me. Then go to the field and do everything yourself since I won't be able to help."

"Oh, no. You're going to pass that test. I know how. Can you sneak out of your house tonight?"

"I don't know. I've never tried and if I get caught I'll be in big trouble.

"But what's your idea?"

"Come over to my house after school and we'll study in the basement until it's time for you to go home. I'll leave the outside basement door unlocked and you can come back after everybody's asleep. Maybe at midnight."

"And we'll study all night."

"Wow," said Harry. "If we get caught, I'll never see my iPad, or you, ever again."

Ginny sighed.

"I know. I'll be grounded until I'm sixteen. But we've got to do it because we're the only ones who know what's going on."

Harry nodded. "See you later, and I hope not for the last time."

4

Chocolate

Harry and Ginny met inside the main entrance of the school the next morning.

"Did you get back to your house without being seen?" asked Ginny.

"Yeah, and I went to several of the hay fields like you suggested and paced them to figure the area. I didn't completely understand what you were telling me last night, but I do now. I'll be okay as long as she doesn't do volume."

"I don't think she will. Mrs. Mills probably thinks that a test on area will get us since we haven't worked on that before. She doesn't know you live on a farm and your dad is always figuring the size of fields."

The next morning Mrs. Mills's face twisted into an evil grin as she passed out the test.

"Ten minutes," she said.

Harry's mouth went dry and he glanced at Ginny who was now on the other side of the room. Mrs. Mills had moved them so they couldn't copy.

Ginny moved her lips to say, "You ... can ... do ... it."

The two friends buried their faces in the paper as the clock ticked. And then, "Time."

The teacher took up the papers and pulled out Harry's and Ginny's. Her face slowly turned red and she stood up and stomped her feet. "You both passed," she said through gritted teeth.

Then she smirked, "Test tomorrow on quadratic equations."

The two left class. Mrs. Mills was not going to do any teaching to a room full of ghosts.

"What are quadratic equations anyway?" asked Harry.

"I'm not sure. Some kind of advanced algebra."

"Makes no difference. Mrs. Mills won't be around to teach tomorrow."

"You know," said Ginny.

"That ghost is really not Mrs. Mills. It acts the complete opposite to the way she does."

"You're right," said Harry. "And do you remember the day that somebody brought a chocolate bar to class? She freaked out. Screamed and told him to get that chocolate out of the room. And Mrs. Mills loves chocolate."

Ginny stopped and grabbed his arm. "Harry ..."

"Are you thinking what I am?" asked Harry.

"Chocolate," said Ginny. "We'll get rid of this ghost with chocolate. That's the only thing it has been afraid of."

"Right. We'll get chocolate to give to Pee Wee and his ghost can smear it on her ghost."

"But Pee Wee was a baseball player. He had a great arm. He can throw the chocolate at her. The store down-town has white chocolate."

Harry grinned. "Great idea. We'll make a baseball out of white chocolate. And he can bean her with it."

"We've got everything figured out," said Ginny.

"Except how to get Mrs. Mills's ghost to the ball field."

Harry scratched his head. "Ghosts don't sleep, right? So what does she do all night? Ghosts usually wander through graveyards, but I bet she wanders through the school."

"That's it," exclaimed Ginny. "And she's probably in the classroom. We'll go and beat on the window and get her to follow us to the ball field."

5

The Ball Field

After school Harry got the bat out of the case and he and Ginny went to the store and bought white chocolate.

They went to her house and microwaved it to make a baseball. Harry even took a knife and carved stitches in it. Harry took the chocolate baseball home with him.

A few minutes before midnight, they met at the ball field.

Harry held up the chocolate baseball and the bat signed by Pee Wee. "Hey, Pee Wee, we've got your bat. The one you used in the pros, and we got a ball."

Nothing happened. Their eyes darted in every direction and they got closer together. The wind blew tufts of fog that swirled around the bases.

“Maybe this wasn’t such a good idea,” stammered Harry.

Then suddenly, right in front of them, a form took shape.

It was the ghost of Pee Wee!

The ghost took the bat and ball, hefted the ball a few times in the air and then said, “What kind of ball is this? It’s so soft it wouldn’t go more than a few feet.”

They took turns explaining to him what had been happening in school. The ghost was shocked.

“What a terrible thing,” he said. “Of course I’ll help you. I can’t imagine why any ghost would do something like this.”

Harry and Ginny hurried to school and on the way worked out a plan to lure the math teacher ghost to the ball field.

They snuck to the window of the classroom. There they saw the ghost furiously doing equations on the white board.

"What's that all about?" asked Harry.

"That ghost really knows math," said Ginny. "What it's writing on the board looks like calculus."

"But why?"

"No idea, but let's get her attention."

They pounded on the window until the ghost came over.

"Go home," she said. "You're not supposed to be here this late."

"We've been watching you do math," said Harry. "You're doing it all wrong. You really don't know much about math, do you?"

The ghost's face got red and she sputtered, "You little twerp. I know more about math than you'll learn in your whole life."

"Then how come we can pass any test that you can give us?" asked Ginny.

"And we know somebody who is so much better than you."

"Who is it?" asked the ghost.

"Come with us," said Harry. "They want to challenge you to a math contest. And we're betting on them."

"We'll see about that," said the ghost as she floated through the wall.

6

In The Basement

Harry and Ginny led her to the ball field where Pee Wee waited.

"This is your expert?" laughed Mrs. Mills's ghost. "He's a baseball player. He knows nothing about math. He never got grades as good as I did."

"Maude?" asked Pee Wee. "Is that you? Why do you look like somebody else?"

"What's going on?" asked Harry.

"This is Maude Hogbottom," said Pee Wee. "She was the best math student in our class and she won many awards."

"Yes," said the ghost. "I was the top math student ever in the school until that one came along."

She pointed at Ginny.

"Why are you doing this?" asked Pee Wee.

"I was peacefully at rest until one night I wandered over to the school and found out that girl, Ginny, was breaking all my math records. All the memories came back. How all of the students, including you, Pee Wee, used to tease me because I was a girl and knew math. It was awful. I decided to teach the whole school a lesson, starting with your class, Miss Ginny. A real math lesson. That those who don't study math are doomed."

"I'm sorry," said Pee Wee. "I didn't realize we treated you so bad. But that was a long time ago. I'm sure kids today don't act like that."

Harry and Ginny secretly exchanged glances and shrugged.

"And, Maude," continued the old baseball player. "You have no right to come back from the dead and harass these children. What did you do with the real Mrs. Mills and the students you changed?"

"I locked them in a room in the basement. Don't worry, there's plenty of food there and a bathroom. I'm the only real ghost and I look like Mrs. Mills because I used her hologram.

"The students are just holograms, too. And I don't care what you think, Pee Wee, I'm glad I did it and I'm going to keep doing it. These two will flunk the test tomorrow, and I'll start on a new class."

"I don't think so," said Pee Wee.

He took the chocolate baseball and tossed it a few times into the air.

"What are you doing?" asked the ghost. "I don't want to play ball with you."

And then the ghost of Maude realized the ball was made of chocolate.

"Chocolate," she screamed. "Get that away from me."

Pee Wee started toward her and she ran towards Harry. Pee Wee flipped the ball to Harry and the ghost turned and ran in another direction. Harry tossed it to Ginny and they had the ghost trapped in a three-way rundown. They closed in and Harry yelled, "Tag her, Pee Wee. "

The ghost of Pee Wee touched the chocolate ball to the ghost of Maude.

There was a poof and the ghostly math teacher vanished.

"She won't bother you anymore," said Pee Wee. "And I hope she's resting peacefully now."

Harry and Ginny stayed with Pee Wee talking baseball and life in Elkton until the sun began to rise and the school opened.

"I have to go," said the ghost of Pee Wee. "Go help your friends and I will go back to my rest. The next time you play ball in the park I may be watching. So play hard, and fair."

The ghost of Pee Wee disappeared and Harry and Ginny ran to the schoolhouse. The outside door had just been opened and they charged down the steps to the basement. They unlocked the door and yanked it open and the students cheered.

They crowded around Harry and Ginny all talking and asking questions. Mrs. Mills asked for quiet and everybody told their story. Then Harry asked, "What are we going to do in class today, Mrs. Mills?"

She scrunched up her face and in a mean voice said, "We're going to have a test."

The class groaned until Mrs. Mills smiled and said, "No, I'm kidding. Actually, we're going to have a class party. And there will be lots of chocolate."

Trapped In Time

1

Something Strange

The school plunged into darkness.

Children screamed, lockers slammed, and teachers pleaded for order.

Percy reached and took Katniss's hand and the two of them eased against the wall out of the way of stumbling students.

"It's still happening," whispered Katniss.

"I was afraid it would be," replied Percy. "The power company never finds anything wrong with the electrical system. We know something else is going on. Something strange."

Katniss squeezed his hand. "Somebody's got to do something. And it looks like it's going to have to be us."

"You got some ideas?"

"Yeah," she said, as the lights flickered and came on. "Can you meet me in the gym after last class?"

"I've got my piano class with Moose right after school. He's only going because I agreed to go, and I don't want to let him down."

"What I have in mind will only take a few minutes."

"I'll be there."

2

The Scratchings

Percy finished his piano lessons and watched Moose pound away on the helpless keyboard with his huge fingers.

Moose so wanted to play the piano, but his thick fingers didn't help. The huge boy thanked Percy for staying with him and Percy took off for the gym.

He had to stop himself from sprinting down the hallway. He held his breath to see what Katniss had come up with, but when he opened the door to the gym, it was empty.

He got a chill.

This whole thing was really weird, he thought, and had been going on way too long. With two months of school left, he hoped Katniss had a good idea. He jumped as he heard a noise above him in the bleachers.

"Hey Perc," hollered Katniss. "Up here."

Percy glanced across the gym at the strange scratchings that had appeared on a concrete wall last week. Nobody knew where they came from, but they were scheduled to be painted over. He climbed up and sat beside Katniss.

"Take a look at that wall," she said pointing across the gym.

"Where the scratchings are?"

"Yeah, look at the scratchings."

Percy squinted. "Wow. It almost seems to be words from up here."

"That's what I thought. Look at the last one."

Percy grabbed her hand. "It says help."

Neither said a word. They just looked at the wall and back at each other.

Finally Katniss spoke, "One of the boys swiped our volleyball and threw it and it bounced all the way up to this corner. He ran away or I would've pounded him. When I got up here I just happened to look over at the marks on the wall. It's definitely writing, but I can't figure out anything except the word 'help.'"

"It just looks like squiggles from the floor," said Percy. "Wait here."

"What are you going to do?"

"I'm going to run down and get the digital camera out of the lab. It has a better zoom than my iPhone. I think they're supposed to paint that wall tomorrow."

Katniss nodded as Percy bounded down the steps.

He returned a few minutes later and they took a number of pictures.

"Now we've got to find a computer and printer with nobody around."

"Why don't you want to tell anyone?" asked Katniss.

"I'm not sure. But I think we need to keep this quiet and see if we can figure out what's going on ourselves. No use panicking everybody. They're scared enough as it is."

The two friends wandered around school and finally found an unused computer and printer in an empty third-grade room.

They closed the door behind them.

"Hurry," said Katniss. "They'll be locking up the school anytime now."

"We can get out a window. I've done it before," said Percy.

"Easy for you to say, and I'm supposed to be home by now. What am I going to tell my mother?"

"You had to study late."

"Percy!"

"You're right. I shouldn't lie. Come on, computer. It's taking forever."

The operating system came up and they downloaded the pictures from the camera. They blew them up on the screen and stared wide-eyed.

"It says," murmured Percy. "'In the basement. Chas Hensley. Help.' What kind of name is Chas?"

"It looks like there's a period after it. I think it's an old time way of writing Charles."

They froze as footsteps sounded in the hall. Katniss let out a breath of relief as the sound went by.

"Print it out and let's get out of here," said Katniss.

"What are you scared of?"

"Mom said if I get into trouble I won't be able to play soccer. And I'm the best player."

"Then you better stay away from me." Percy grinned.

Katniss smacked him on the shoulder as the printer spit out the photos. They grabbed the papers and beat the guard to the door.

"Now what?" asked Percy as they walked home.

"Let's go to the library tonight and use their computers to look up Charles Hensley."

"I hate those computers," grumbled Percy. "They block all the good sites."

"You mean the bad sites. There's a lot of stuff out there you shouldn't see, Perc."

"Come on Kat. I'm almost twelve. There's not much I don't know."

Katniss snickered. "Yeah, Percy Johnson, smartest person in the world and only twelve-years-old."

"Stuff it, Kat. I'll meet you at seven. And what are you going to tell your mom?"

"I'll tell her I have to meet you to study and ..."

Percy laughed.

"Percy," stammered Katniss. "I do have to study and I can do that while we search."

"Whatever," said Percy.

3

The Missing Scientist

At seven that evening the two sixth graders crowded together peering at a computer screen. They searched, over and over, the name Charles Hensley, but nothing came up that seemed to fit their school. As Katniss studied, Percy tried more searches. Then she slammed her book shut and jumped up. "I got an idea."

She hurried to the librarian and asked where she could find a list of all the students who had ever attended their elementary school. The librarian directed her to a filing cabinet that contained much of the history of the school. Percy joined her and they started an exhausting search of the records.

"Why do you think Charles Hensley was a student?" asked Percy.

"Just a hunch. We haven't heard of anything else happening around town.

I figured since the weirdness is at school, it has to be a former student."

"I'll buy that. Good thinking."

Thirty minutes before closing time, Percy let out a yell, "I found him!"

As the librarian shushed Percy, Katniss looked over his shoulder. They saw a fourth grade boy wearing glasses with unruly hair sticking straight up.

"Charles looks like a nerd," said Percy.

"He's adorable. But he does look like he's pretty smart."

She pulled the class picture out of the file and took it to the librarian.

"How can we find information about this boy?"

The librarian looked down through her bifocals at the boy. "Charles Hensley," she said. "I know that name. Search the records of the old local newspaper. It's scanned in online."

She gave them the link to the newspaper's archive. It didn't take them long to find an article about Charles Hensley.

It was copied from the New York Times and said that scientist Charles Hensley had gone missing. His wife reported that he had gone to his workshop the night before with plans to work all night on a new invention.

He had left her a letter on the dining room table. He had not been seen since, and no body had been found. Most scientists were dismissive of Hensley's work and some made fun of him. The paper went on to say that the man had been born and raised here and went to the elementary school there.

Percy's hand shook as he wrote down the information in a notebook. "Kat, this story is from 1953. How can Charles be the one that wrote on the wall?"

"I've been thinking about all this. There's somebody out there, maybe Charles, who is trying to tell us something. But why doesn't he or she just walk up and talk to us? Obviously, they can't. It's almost like they're trapped somewhere and can't get to us."

"Like a ghost?"

"I don't think so," said Katniss.

"How could we help a ghost? They're dead. And I don't believe in goofy ghosts anyway."

"So where is Charles?"

"I think he's stuck in another time."

"That's crazy, Kat. Are you talking about time travel, like in a *Wrinkle in Time*?"

"I don't know. But it has to be something like that."

Katniss jumped up and went back to the librarian. "How can we find information about this man's family?"

"Folks around here do that all the time," she said. "Look in ancestry.com. If you need a password the library has one you can use."

"Kat," said Percy. "You're finding out all kinds of stuff from the librarian."

"Sure, unlike you, librarians really do know everything, or at least where to find it."

Percy rolled his eyes at her and pulled up the website. They quickly found information on Charles Hensley. The date he disappeared, and the name of his wife and daughter were listed on the site.

Also the letter that the New York Times referred to had been scanned in. They held their breath as they read it.

4

Trapped In Time

March 5, 1953

My most dearest Rebecca,

I've done it. I've really done it. I discovered the way to go back into time. This is an accumulation of my life's work. All the laughter, all the sneers, all the doubts, that I heard from so many people so many times, now have no meaning. I will be famous and rich.

Finally, my dearest, we will be able to take our long-delayed European honeymoon that we have planned for so many years.

I know there were times when you doubted me, but you stood by me when no one else would. You have been and will always be my dearest love.

Tonight I will take my first experimental trip. I intend to go back to the old school in Kentucky where I was raised before I came to New York.

I'm hoping that I might get a glimpse of my parents as children and finally see my grandparents who died before I was born.

The excitement is almost more than I can stand. What wonderful stories I will be able to tell you tomorrow.

Dream of me tonight, my love, and I will meet you tomorrow for our usual lunchtime.

All my love from your greatest admirer,

Charles

Percy took a deep breath, "He never made it for lunch. You were right, Kat."

"Because he's still in the old school and it has been torn down," Katniss said, with a sniffle.

"We're going to do something about it," said Percy.

"Yeah," said Katniss. "But how do we get someone out of a school that no longer exists and who is in another time?"

Their thoughts were interrupted by the librarian saying, "Closing time."

On the way home they mulled over a variety of ideas, but couldn't find an answer.

The next morning the school was abuzz with excitement.

Another scratching had been found on a wall. This time it was in the girls' bathroom and they were all freaked out about it.

Girls were asking each other how someone snuck into their bathroom without being seen and they wondered if it was a boy.

Katniss and Percy knew and agreed to meet in the hallway between classes.

"Could you tell what it said?" asked Percy.

"Yeah, it's clear this time. Everybody can see it. It says 'locket'"

"Locket? What does that mean?"

"I don't know," said Katniss. "But I'll meet you at the library again tonight at seven."

Percy nodded as the bell rang.

5

The Locket

"There it is," said Percy.

The image on the library computer screen showed a thin gold chain with an oval shaped locket dangling on the end. The information said that the image had been uploaded by the daughter of Rebecca Hensley upon the death of her mother.

The locket had been given as a wedding gift to her mother by her father.

"But where is it now?" asked Katniss.

Percy scrolled down and the two gasped.

"OMG," exclaimed Katniss.

"It's here."

The article stated that the daughter donated the locket to the Kentucky town where her father had been born and grew up.

"But where?" asked Percy.

There was no more information in the article. Katniss went to the librarian who said she didn't know anything about it.

"But let me make a call," the woman said. "Somebody in town will know."

She called the number and as Katniss and Percy watched, her eyes grew wide.

"Here?" she asked.

She hung up the phone and faced the two friends.

"It's stored in the library. No one in town could figure out a place to display it, so it's in a cabinet in the back room."

"Can we see it?" asked Percy, a bit too eagerly.

The librarian rubbed her chin. "I guess so. This is for a class project, right?"

"Yes," said Katniss. "We're trying to find out about Charles Hensley. The school really needs to know about him."

Percy stared at her with a sly grin.

The librarian took them to a back room.

She opened an old wooden cabinet.

She searched around at the bottom of the cabinet and brought out a metal box. She gently opened the top and there, wrapped in cloth, was the locket. The gold had tarnished, but they could see it was once a beautiful piece of jewelry.

"Can we borrow it?" asked Percy.

"Oh no," said the librarian. "We couldn't allow this to be taken out of the building. If you'd like to take pictures of it, you're welcome to do so."

Percy pulled out his phone and took a few snapshots. As the librarian bent over to put the box back into the cabinet, Percy tiptoed to the window and unlocked it.

Katniss shook her head. She knew what he had planned.

The two went back into the main library and sat in a corner.

"You're planning to come back and steal that aren't you?" asked Katniss.

"Not steal, borrow," Percy said.

"Percy," she said. "That's against the law.

"You can't break into the library and take the lock-et. That's stealing. They'll put you in jail."

"We'll just take it for a few hours and bring it back later. Nobody will miss it. They didn't even know it was here."

Katniss shook her head.

"Then what do you suggest? Unless you have a better idea, I'm coming back tonight and getting the locket."

"And then what? You don't know where Mr. Hensley is. And how are you going to get the locket to him? He's in another time."

Percy looked at his hands. "There has to be a way."

"Let's ask him."

Percy looked up. "Ask him? How?"

"I think he knows we're trying to help him. Let's go to school early in the morning and ask him where he is and what we should do.

"You go to the gym and ask out loud and I'll go to the girls' bathroom.

"Maybe he'll write something on the wall."

Percy shrugged. “Might as well. I don’t know what else to do.”

6

Message

The next morning they got to school when the doors first opened. Percy hurried to the gym and Katniss ducked into the girls' bathroom.

Both places were empty. Separately, they each spoke out loud with the hope that Charles Hensley could somehow hear them. Nothing happened, and they went to their classes.

At lunchtime the school was buzzing again. More scratchings had been seen. This time in the cafeteria.

Percy and Katniss met for lunch and, with several other kids, wandered over to the scratchings.

"I can't read it," said Percy. "But it has to be a message for us."

"I can't either, but you're right."

They looked at it from several different directions, but it didn't seem to make sense.

Katniss plopped down in a chair.,

"Take your notepad and write down as best you can what you see. And I'll do the same."

They both walked around the scratchings with their notepads writing down what they thought they saw. They found an empty lunch table and took their trays and sat down. They scooted together and compared notes.

"I think we got it," said Katniss.

"Yeah. That was a good idea to write it down. The first word does look like CAFE. And the second is BRI."

"And the third," said Katniss. "Is LOCK."

"But what does it mean?"

"How about cafeteria, bring locket."

"That's it, but I don't think he means this cafeteria," said Percy.

"Then he's in the cafeteria of the old school. Except it doesn't exist anymore."

"It does," said Percy.

"What are you talking about?"

"My dad told me that when they tore down the old school to build this one, they didn't fill in the basement, just covered it over. It's out in the woods behind the school somewhere."

"Did he say what was in the basement?"

"The cafeteria."

7

Steal, Or Borrow?

That afternoon after school Percy and Katniss scoured the woods looking for the old basement. Percy's dad had told him about where it was, but they couldn't find it.

Then Katniss stopped. "Turn around, Perc. Look behind us."

"That's it," he said. "We walked right over it. Twice. But you can see a mound from here. It's higher than the rest of the forest floor."

They walked around the mound trying to find some kind of opening. Percy suddenly stopped and got down on his hands and knees. He grabbed a small rock and pulled it away from the mound. Behind it was an opening.

"I bet this is a way in," he said. "But it's too small, and the other rocks around it are too big to move."

He stuck his hand in the hole and slapped upward.

"Look at that. It's concrete. This was the ceiling of the basement and it's still intact."

"But how are we going to move those rocks?" asked Katniss. "It would take somebody as big as a ..."

"Moose!" They both said together and laughed.

"Moose is still at school doing extra work so he can stay on the football team. I'll ask him if he can help us."

"Why does Moose have to do makeup work?" asked Katniss. "He's smart and gets good grades."

"His father said he can't play football unless he gets straight A's."

"Well, I hope he does. He really helps the football team because he's so big."

"Kat, he is the football team."

She laughed. "Yeah, I guess so. He can play any position and when he's got the ball nobody can stop him. I've never seen a twelve-year-old kid as big as he is."

"Yeah, they weren't going to let him play at first because they were afraid he'd hurt some of the smaller kids.

"But he's real gentle and careful not to hurt anybody. He's my best friend ... after you, I mean."

Katniss smiled and shook her head at him. "I have to get home. When are we going to try to get in there?"

"If Moose can do it, tonight. We can tell our parents we're going to the library again."

"Percy, I've told you I don't want to lie to my parents. And, oh ... we still need the locket."

"Right. As soon as the librarian leaves, I'll sneak in and get it."

"No! You can't break in and steal it."

"I told you, I'm not stealing it. I'm borrowing it. I'll take it back. And besides, it belongs to Mr. Hensley."

"His daughter gave it to the city. It's theirs, and you'll have to get permission to use it. I'm not going to be friends with a thief."

"Come on, Katniss. Nobody's going to let us take the locket. Here's what we'll do. We'll tell our parents we're going to the library to study until it closes and we will. Then, I'll get the locket and we'll meet Moose at the mound.

"You know nobody's going to believe us if we tell them there's some crazy scientist stuck in time in the basement of the old school."

"I don't care. If you steal that locket I don't want to ever see you again."

"Aw, Katniss, don't be that way."

She stomped off and Percy hollered as she walked away, "Moose and I are going to be at the old school tonight with the locket to give it to its rightful owner. Please come with us."

Katniss didn't answer and Percy stuck his hands in his pockets and went to find Moose.

8

Moose's Secret

Percy met Moose walking across the field beside the school. He told his big friend about Mr. Hensley and that he needed help to move rocks and get inside the old basement. Moose said no.

"Why, Moose?" asked Percy.

"I'm just not going to do it."

Percy threw up his hands. "Darn it. You and Katniss. Moose, we've got to help Mr. Hensley. Nobody else can do it, just us. I can get the locket, but I can't get into the old school. Please help."

Moose shook his head.

"But you're my friend. Or, I thought you were."

"I still am." Moose lifted him off the ground and held him in a bear hug. Percy tried to get away.

"Stop, Moose. You know I don't like you hugging me, especially in public. Let me go."

Moose released his grip and Percy fell to the ground. "Why, Moose. Why won't you do this? It's really important and I need you."

Moose sat down beside him. "If I tell you, you have to promise not to ever tell anybody."

"You know I'd never tell. What's going on?"

The big kid drew circles in the dirt with his finger. "I'm afraid of dark places. I can't go in caves and stuff like that. I couldn't ever go into an old, dark, nasty basement."

"I didn't think you were afraid of anything. But it's okay. We're all afraid of something. If you go with me and help me move the rock, then you can wait outside."

Moose nodded. "I can do that. I'll meet you at the edge of the woods. And, Percy, this could be dangerous. You'll have to be very careful."

9

Into The Basement

Percy eased the window open. The librarian had been gone long enough that he felt she wouldn't be coming back for anything. He figured the window would still be open. After all, who would ever break into a library? Well, he just did.

Katniss's warning rang in his ears. He could go to jail for this. But he wasn't too worried. This was a small town after all and everybody knew his family. They really wouldn't lock him up, but still, his heart pounded against his rib cage as he bent over and pulled out the box. He had brought a zip lock bag from home and he slid the locket into it. He replaced the box in the cabinet. As he started back towards the window, he saw movement. He froze in terror. A voice hissed at him,

"Hand it out to me."

He knew the voice.

"Kat, Is that you?" he whispered.

"Who did you think it would be, pea brain?"

"But I thought ..."

"Shush, and come on."

He handed her the locket and climbed out the window, closing it quietly behind him. He started to ask another question, but she shushed him again. They snuck through back yards and through tree lines without saying a word until they reached the forest. A giant hulk was silhouetted against the sky.

"Moose?" murmured Percy.

"Yeah, hurry up. I have to get home before dad finds I'm gone. I snuck out a window."

"We're all going to be in trouble," said Katniss. "But you're right Percy, we have to do this. We have to help Mr. Hensley."

She put her arm around his shoulder.

Percy clicked on a flashlight then led the group to the mound and located the hole. He had replaced the rock he removed to hide the opening. He pulled it away and grabbed another one.

"Help me, Moose."

Moose grabbed the other side and effortlessly took the rock out of the hole.

"One more," said Percy.

This time Katniss helped and the three of them moved an even bigger rock. There was plenty of room now for them to get into the basement.

"You two stay here," said Percy. "I'll go down and see if there's some way I can contact Mr. Hensley."

"Oh, no," said Katniss. "We're going down, too. It's too dangerous for you to go down there alone. Right Moose?"

"No," said Percy. "We'll need at least one person up here to watch in case somebody comes. If you want to go down with me, Kat, come on."

"We may need Moose to help us in there."

"I'll go," said Moose. His voice cracked.

"No, you don't have ...," started Percy.

"I'll go."

Percy went first. As they lowered themselves into the hole, Moose gave out a soft moan.

"Are you okay, Moose?" asked Katniss.

"He's fine," said Percy. "He has some allergies and this place is full of dust and mold."

"Are you sure," said Katniss, "that he's ..."

"Look," Percy interrupted. "There are still some old tables and chairs down here from the cafeteria."

"Who cares," said Katniss. "How are we going to find Mr. Hensley?"

"Like we did before. We'll talk to him."

Percy took out the plastic bag and pulled the locket out of it. He held it up with one hand and shined his light on it with the other.

"Mr. Hensley," he called. "We're here. We have the locket."

"What do you want us to do?" asked Katniss.

10

Charles Hensley

A dust-filled chair in the corner moved slightly. They all jumped.

"He's here," mumbled Katniss. "He's here."

Percy called again, "Charles Hensley. The locket that you gave to Rebecca is here."

The locket, dangling from Percy's hand, vibrated slightly. Katniss grabbed Percy's arm.

"You're close, Mr. Hensley," said Katniss. "Come to us. It's Rebecca's locket. The woman you love most in all the world."

The chain shook again and fingers, from out of nowhere, enclosed the oval-shaped locket. Percy gasped, but didn't move as Katniss let out a soft "OMG."

Moose whimpered.

The fingers tightly squeezed the locket as another hand appeared and gripped the chain.

Katniss said, "Come on, Mr. Hensley. You're here."

Part of a leg appeared. Then a foot, and, suddenly, a man stood before them.

He was a man in his twenties wearing a suit and a fedora hat. He blinked at the light shining in his face.

"Where am I?" he asked.

"You're in the basement of the old elementary school," replied Percy.

The man squinted into the darkness at the dingy room. "What year is this?"

"2019," said Katniss.

Mr. Hensley grabbed Percy's shoulder to keep from falling. "That can't be," he said. "I only left a few days ago."

"It's true," said Percy. "What happened to you in the past? What did you see?"

"Not much. I ended up in the cafeteria of my old school in 1938, but I couldn't leave. And every day was the same. The same children came to eat and said the same things. Over and over."

"Like *Groundhog Day*," said Percy.

"I saw that old movie," said Moose. "It was awes ..."

"Shut up, you two," interrupted Katniss. "Mr. Hensley doesn't care about a dumb movie. How did you send us the messages?"

"I knew from my experiments that different times exist side-by-side. I concentrated on trying to get to another one. But I couldn't. I did see shadows, shapes, and heard voices. I managed to get my hand through a few times and scratch a message on a wall with a fork."

"We saw them," said Katniss. "And you made the lights go off. We're the ones who asked you questions."

"I'm so glad I heard you. Thank you. I knew the locket would help me break through the time continuum. I didn't know if you would be able to find it."

"Your daughter donated it to the town after your wife died," said Percy.

Katniss shoved Percy. "Big mouth. You shouldn't have said that."

"It's all right," said Mr. Hensley. "My wife is still alive in 1953 and I'm going back. And it's good to know I'll have a daughter. Can we go now?"

"I need to get back to New York and my machine."

Percy shined his light toward the opening just as a rock fell from above. Then another one. Then the entire opening collapsed with rocks and dirt flowing into the dust-filled basement.

They were trapped!

11

Escape

When the dust settled, they walked around the pile of rock. There was no way out. Moose dropped to his hands and knees and crawled away from the rock to a corner where he buried his face in his hands.

"Moose," said Percy. "Are you okay?"

The big kid didn't reply. He only made groaning sounds.

"Moose," said Percy. "We need you. You're the strongest one here and the only one who can move all that rock. I know you're afraid, Moose, and that's okay. But we could die here without you."

Percy got down beside Moose and put his arms around his friend. He patted the big boy on the back and said, "Moose, you've always been my friend and you'll always be my friend. You can do this."

Moose turned and looked at the rocks.

He pushed himself up and bellowed like ... well, a moose. And he attacked the pile of debris. Rocks flew one after another as Moose tore into the mound. Katniss joined him and handed rocks to Percy who passed them to Mr. Hensley.

After an hour they all sat down to rest except Moose. He grabbed rock after rock and with a loud grunt tossed it to the side. For every rock he moved, another fell to replace it, but he never hesitated.

After the other three had rested, they rejoined Moose and as he lifted an especially big rock, the rocks above shifted down and a hole at the top appeared. Through the hole they saw—night sky.

The four scrambled up into the fresh air. Mr. Hensley waved his arms in joy and said, "Tell me how I can get to New York."

"If you can get to the Army base, you can catch a bus to almost anywhere," said Katniss.

"I've got an old bike," said Moose. "You can have it. I keep it behind the school."

"Thank you," said the man.

"But I don't know the route to the base."

Percy took out his iPhone and pulled up a map. Mr. Hensley took the iPhone with shaking hands.

"This is the most amazing thing I have ever seen," he said. "I hope I live long enough to be able to use one of these."

"We can even see your house in New York," said Percy. "I just need the address."

Mr. Hensley gave it to him and Percy pulled up street view.

The man almost dropped the iPhone. "My laboratory," he gasped. "It's gone. There's another building there now. What happened to my machine?"

The three friends didn't know what to say. Moose put his arm around the man. "Maybe it's still there."

"You're right," said Mr. Hensley. "My machine was in the subbasement. They might not have known it was even there when they built the new house."

Moose got his bicycle and the scientist climbed on. He handed Percy the locket.

"Put this back where you found it.

"My daughter will some day donate it to the town. Otherwise, it would simply disappear."

Percy slid it back into the plastic bag.

"Thank you so much," Mr. Hensley said. "If my machine is there and I'm able to get back to my time, I'll try to come and visit you. I'll be an old man then."

The man who had been trapped in time rode into the darkness.

Epilogue

As Moose, Percy, and Katniss walked toward the parking lot, Percy said, "Only three more days until school's out. I can't wait."

"We'll have fun this summer," said Katniss.

"Look at that," said Moose. "Some old dude standing by his car is waving at us."

"Don't go near him," said Percy. "Might be some kind of weirdo."

Katniss started running toward the stranger.

"Stop her, Moose," screamed Percy.

They ran after her. She got to the man first and threw her arms around him.

"It's Mr. Hensley," she said. They crowded around him and he hugged them all.

"I told you I'd come back," he said. "My machine was still there. It was rusty and needed work, but I got it going and went back home.

"Then I destroyed the machine. It was too dangerous. But my scientific work made me a very wealthy man. And I have something for you."

He handed each one of them an envelope. "In there," he said, "is information I sent to the school about scholarships to the college of your choice. They won't know who it came from unless you tell them. It's the least I can do after what you did for me."

The three friends smiled and pumped his hand up and down.

"Wow," said Percy. "I never thought I'd get a chance to go to college. Thanks, Mr. Hensley."

The others nodded their agreement.

With one last goodbye, the old scientist got back in the car and drove away.

"Ah, good *times*," said Percy, with a grin.

Katniss and Moose both pounded him on the arm.

Saving Millie

Chapter One

Lonely

The eye.

The close up of the single eye gave Jane goosebumps.

"Aww, that whale is so sad and lonely," said Jane to the other girls watching the television.

Charlotte hooted. "Now, Jane, oops, I mean *Isabella*, can read the mind of a beached whale."

Jane glared at Charlotte, her nemesis, who always made fun of her.

Jane did exaggerate some, well, maybe a lot, but that was no reason to be mean.

"Why do you think the whale is lonely?" asked one of the other girls.

"I just feel it."

"Like you feel an English prince is coming to adopt you?" said Charlotte.

Charlotte got up and changed the channel. "The whale is dead. Beached whales never survive."

"And all your dreams about it are as dumb as your dreams about getting adopted. Nobody will adopt us. We're all too old."

Jane pushed herself off the couch and left the TV room. She did have dreams. She wanted someday to have a family with real parents, not paid lackeys. She wanted to be called Isabella, not Jane. What was wrong with that? Nobody knew what her real name was. She was left at the orphanage as a baby and called Jane. She hated it.

But at least this orphanage didn't mistreat the kids like some she'd heard about. She didn't like the food, but they had plenty, and the staff was okay. Especially Mrs. Dodson. She sometimes called Jane, Isabella.

And since Jane had turned ten, she could sign out, and go out into the neighborhood.

The orphans' building was in a bad part of town, but during the day the older children, in pairs, could walk to the library, or to the park. Not that there was anything in the park. A few broken swings and a lopsided, rotting seesaw.

But at least there was a little scraggly grass and some pitiful looking trees. A small oasis in the bleakness of the city. A place to escape. Away from the noise and the chaos for an hour or so.

But the library.

That was Jane's favorite place. The old building reeked with the smells of mold, dust, and urine from the toilets that didn't work, but to the girl, it was a palace. A palace of words, and ideas, and adventures. Where, for a while, she could forget who and where she was.

And at the library she could learn more about whales and dolphins. She loved these big mammals and had actually seen an injured dolphin on a field trip to the New Orleans aquarium.

Jane had begged to go back, but Mrs. Dodson said the trip had been paid for by a special grant that they wouldn't get again.

Once a month, in good weather, the older kids would have a field trip to a park overlooking the river. The Mississippi River. Grass grew everywhere.

Real grass. Green grass. Grass that felt cool in her hands and smelled like outdoors and freedom.

Jane would lie in it, picking the stalks and tossing them into the wind. The green shoots soared over the field all the way to the river and disappeared. Like all of her dreams and hopes.

She'd walk to the bluff overlooking the river and watch the boats and barges chug up and down the muddy water. Sometimes a paddle wheel passenger boat would churn by boiling the water and making waves. Kids would sometimes wave at her, but she never waved back. She wanted to be there with them.

Chapter Two
Save the Whale

That afternoon, after a day of chores, Jane went back to the TV room and turned on the New Orleans news. No one else was around and the beached whale was again the top story. Jane knelt in front of the TV.

Again she was drawn to the whale's eye. She remembered the eyes of the dolphin in New Orleans and how she felt like it was trying to tell her something. Like get me out of this giant, glass cage. It wanted to be back in its home in the Gulf of Mexico.

Jane told the animal that it could go back as soon as it was better. And not long after that, she read in the newspaper that the aquarium took the dolphin back to the Gulf of Mexico. She never forgot looking into that dolphin's eyes and knowing its thoughts.

The whale had beached itself on a spit of land south of New Orleans called Grand Isle. The news said whale experts were coming and that they would try to pull the whale back into the ocean.

But I'm the only one that can save the whale, she thought. I know how it feels. And what it needs.

She had to figure out a way to get to the whale. And her method of finding things out was to go to the library. After getting permission from Mrs. Dodson, she and another girl left the orphanage and headed towards the library.

The setting sun glinted on dirty windows and strewn broken glass in this rundown neighborhood, but Jane didn't notice. All of her thoughts were focused on getting to New Orleans.

She did spot the three boys who hung out on the corner across from the library. They always seemed to be there, but never bothered her—except to stare.

Once one of them had hollered at her, but the tallest one said, "Knock it off."

At the library she went straight to her favorite librarian, Ms. Amanda. The woman always had a ready smile for Jane.

"Hi, Ms. Amanda," she said. "I was watching the news today and saw a whale on a beach in New Orleans."

The woman nodded, "I saw that, too"

"I want to find out more about it and look at some maps to see where it actually is."

Ms. Amanda got up from her chair, and said, "We can do that. Come with me."

Jane spent the hour that she was allowed to be away from the orphanage finding the island where the whale had beached and a way to get there.

She discovered that no Greyhound buses went there. And how would she get money for a bus anyway?

Then she thought of the river.

Boats went to New Orleans. And maybe to Grand Isle. Jane thought of the paddlewheel boats and of all the kids on them. She could sneak on a boat.

What a way to go to New Orleans. In style with fancy meals and a view of the river.

Her daydream took her to a classy dining room with mounds of food everywhere and waiters bringing it all to her.

On the internet, she checked the schedules of passenger boats going from Baton Rouge to New Orleans.

None went to Grand Isle but they did have tours there from New Orleans.

A boat would be leaving from Baton Rouge in the morning. She would be on that boat. Jane wasn't sure how, but she would.

Really this time.

No made up dream. She had to go.

Because of the whale.

It would be fun, and besides, what's the worst that could happen?

Chapter Three

Dark Night

Late that night, Jane sat up in bed. She had planned to wake up in the middle of the night to leave. She slipped out of bed and crept to the hall to check the clock. Three o'clock. Perfect.

Jane had packed her backpack earlier and hidden it under her bed. Now the trick was to get out of the orphanage. She knew all the doors were alarmed, but her idea was to go out a window.

She slept on the second floor and there was an old heavy-duty downspout right outside the window in the bathroom. She thought she could climb down that way. It would be dangerous she knew, but the whale needed her.

Nobody else ever had.

Jane eased her raggedy backpack out from under the bed and tiptoed toward the bathroom. She knew where every squeaky board was. And if anyone woke up she would only be going to the bathroom.

But with a backpack? She'd have to invent a story, but she was good at that.

She didn't make a sound and closed the bathroom door behind her.

The window was open. But it did have a screen. Fastened with a hook. She unlatched it and tried to push it out of the way. It was hinged at the top and she couldn't find a way to get it loose. She would have to get out with the screen banging against her back.

She had planned to climb down the downspout with her backpack on, but she didn't think she could get through the window that way. So she had to drop it. There was enough light outside from the streetlights that she could see the ground. She aimed the backpack for a bush just off to her left. It hit square in the middle, but still made a sound.

She waited. Listening for any kind of movement in the building. After a few minutes she turned around and put her feet out the window hanging onto the sill. Her left hand inched its way toward the downspout.

Oh please, oh please, she thought, don't let it break.

She held on with her right hand and moved her left hand to the downspout grabbing one of the downspout's supports and then quickly moved her right hand beside it.

The screen scratched her back and banged her head, but she got out. Now all she had to do was get down.

The distance between the supports was further away than her legs could reach. So she'd have to slide. Her heart pounded like the jackhammers she heard working on the street. If she fell, she'd go so deep into the old muddy dirt they wouldn't have to bury her.

Slowly, carefully, she eased herself down with her feet stopping at each support so she could get a breath until finally her beat up tennis shoes touched the ground.

She crawled over to the bush, got her backpack, and lay there gasping for breath. Her hands shook both from fear and the strain of hanging on so long, but she had done it. She was on her way to save the whale.

The night was as black as the depths of a coal mine. Only a few streetlights made circles of light in the dingy streets. Her whole body tensed as she reached the sidewalk. Jane had never been out in the city at this time of night.

Her eyes darted in all directions.

She should not be here, alone, on the dangerous streets of Baton Rouge.

But the whale.

The only thing besides fear on her mind.

She kept in the shadows with her eyes watching for any kind of movement, but only a scraggly stray cat was on the streets with her.

Broken glass littered the streets glinting like monster eyes in the light of the few working street lights. Soon these imagined monsters might be devouring her—one limb at a time.

As she rounded a corner, she heard voices. Male voices. Three boys were coming towards her on the opposite side of the street.

They looked like the same ones that stared at her on her way to the library. She ducked between several metal trash cans and her body froze.

“Hey,” shouted one. "I saw something move on the other side of the street.”

“I'll go check,” said another.

Chapter Four

Climbing Aboard

Jane shook with fear. Should she run? No, they could easily catch her. She tried to make herself as small as possible behind one of the trash cans, but the man, actually the tall boy, immediately saw her. He stared for a minute and then hollered to the others, "Ain't nothing, but an old alley cat."

Jane mouthed the words "thank you."

The boys moved on down the street, kicking trash cans and shoving each other.

Jane crept from her hiding place and resumed her scary journey.

She was more careful now, her eyes and ears straining for any sound or movement. But she covered the last few blocks to the river with its docks and wharves without any further trouble.

She had found the schedule of the commercial riverboats that plied the Mississippi River and the one she wanted floated at the dock glowing in its deck lights.

The lights and colors reminded Jane of a carnival. Her hands got sweaty with excitement.

There were two gangways, one at the back and one at the front and each had a guard. A few workers milled around the wharf area. Most passengers wouldn't show up until later in the morning, but one family did go on board and the guards checked everyone's ticket. She couldn't just lie her way on.

The girl had thought about sneaking on by blending into a family with kids. She didn't have much hope that would work now. No, she had to figure out something else. Before daylight and before the crowds. But it looked hopeless.

Jane followed shadows and edged down to the water where she crouched behind a stanchion away from the back of the ship. She had thought about trying to climb up the mooring ropes, but they were bathed with light and had a cone-shaped object on them. She knew that was to prevent rats from climbing the ropes onto the ship. Then she noticed a single rope hanging down into the water.

That would be perfect, she thought, except it also was in the light and she could be seen climbing up the ship by anybody standing on the dock.

But what about on the other side of the ship? The dark side. There might be a rope, but she'd have to swim in the dark, muddy Mississippi River to find out. She wondered if sharks came this far up the river or if there were giant girl-eating catfish.

More than likely there was pollution that could make her barf for a week if she got a mouth full of water.

Jane dug through her backpack looking for shorts. The only clothes she had were the jeans she had on, the shorts and, stuffed away at the bottom of the pack, one carefully folded dress she had gotten from the local Goodwill.

And, oh how she loved that dress. It looked brand-new when she got it, but now it was beginning to get a bit ragged. She wore the flower-covered dress every time she went to the library.

A rich lady once came to the orphanage and took

the older girls to Goodwill and bought them clothes.

Jane hoped she could find a place to change into the dress thinking she wouldn't look quite so much like what she was. An orphan.

She found her shorts and hid behind the stanchion and changed. Then she folded her jeans, putting them in the backpack. The shorts and T-shirts could get wet, but she had a big garbage bag she snuck out of the kitchen.

If she put her backpack inside the garbage bag that would keep everything dry and keep her afloat.

She grinned. Everything was working out. As long as there was another rope on the other side. Big if. But she had to try. She couldn't think of anything else.

She eased herself into the water desperately trying not to get any on her face. She knew how dirty the Mississippi was and drinking just a few drops would probably make her sick. She floated slowly kicking and paddling as quietly as she could past the stern of the boat to the other side. There was a flexible rope ladder. It didn't go down to the water.

But she thought she could reach it. She paddled up to the ladder.

Jane would have to take her backpack out of the garbage bag so she could use both hands to climb. She wasn't sure how to do that.

As she treaded water, something brushed against her leg. She jumped and grabbed the ladder and dangled by one hand with her legs curled up.

A warm dribble streamed down her leg.

No, she thought, I'm way too old. Imagine what the girls would say.

Oh, well, that was one way to do it. The fish, or whatever it was, probably wouldn't hurt her, but who knows, it might have been a hammerhead.

Jane stuck both legs through a rung in the rope ladder and looped one hand around another rung giving her the use of both hands to open the plastic bag. She wrapped herself around the ladder like an octopus as she opened the bag and pulled out the backpack.

The girl thought about throwing the bag into the water, but it would end up as part of the tons of plastic fouling the ocean, so she wadded it up and stuck it in the waistband of her shorts.

Hanging on with one hand and balancing on the ladder rung Jane managed to get the backpack on her back and climbed up toward the dark, spooky side of the boat.

Chapter Five

On the Boat

Now what? Jane thought. If they caught her sneaking onto the boat she'd be back in the orphanage, or worse —in Juvie. But she had no choice. So she climbed like she did the rock wall at the playground and reached the top.

She heard voices in the distance, but this side of the boat appeared empty. Shadow and light played across the deck like a piano keyboard. Each dark spot could hide a sailor who would put her in leg irons in a dark, dank brig.

Above her was the upper part of the ship with windows looking down. Who could be watching her there? Kidnappers?

Still crunched down on the rope she took off her backpack and put it over the railing. She climbed up and flopped to the floor.

Jane crawled pulling her backpack behind her trying to stay in the dark. Jane desperately needed a place to hide, but had no idea what was on the boat. Maybe a closet or some kind of room not being used, but she didn't think that was likely.

She got away from the windows and was hidden in darkness. A small light glowed above a closed door. A place to hide or a room full of unsavory sailors? Might as well find out.

Jane crawled to the door and grasped the handle. It wouldn't move.

She set down her backpack and threw her entire weight against it.

The latch clicked, and she slowly opened the door hoping to prevent an ear-shattering noise that would send her back to the orphanage.

Inch by inch she opened it until it was wide enough for her to squeeze in. She felt around and found a light switch and shut the door before turning it on.

A room full of machinery filled her eyes, and with a place for her to lie down. Good enough for tonight, she thought. She curled up in a corner behind a small machine that looked like a motor.

Jane hoped it didn't come on in the night and rip her body to shreds.

The metal floor dug into her hips,

And her mind drifted to her bed in the orphanage as she went right to sleep dreaming of whales.

Chapter Six

Dalmar

She jerked awake as the door squealed open and the light flashed on. Jane grabbed her things and scurried into the shadows.

She peeked around the metal cowling of a machine to see the man squirting something into holes in a larger machine. Grease?

He turned toward her. Jane rolled herself into a ball and wiggled under the metal monster hoping there were no grease holes in the bottom.

The squishy, squishy sound came closer. Her clothes shook from her pounding heart.

And then he was gone and the room dark again.

Jane crawled out from her hiding place and turned on the light. Her shorts and top were a mess. Covered with grease and dirt. So were her arms and legs. She couldn't put on her nice dress when she was filthy.

And going out in dirty shorts and shirt wasn't an option.

She wandered around the small space desperately searching for something to use to clean up. And she found it.

A water faucet. It was connected to a short hose and she pulled off her T-shirt, hoping no one would come in, and used it to scrub herself. The shirt was ruined, but she had gotten herself mostly clean. At least now she could put on her good dress and try to find a ladies room.

She cracked open the door to see bright sunshine and hear voices mixed with laughter.

She didn't want someone to see her coming out of this room. That would definitely cause suspicion, but people were everywhere. At that moment, the band began playing on the dock. Everyone went to the railing to take a look. Jane snuck out quickly and joined them. A band was marching across the dock and up the gangplank onto the boat. What a great time to explore with everyone milling about.

She strolled to the bow of the ship trying to look like she belonged. She wasn't sure how to act like a rich, fancy girl, but she held her head high and put a sway in her walk. She stopped at the railing and stared in awe.

The brown beast of water churned and rolled heading South to the Gulf. A statuary of herons lined the shallows waiting for food. And a misty fog curled itself around gnarled stumps.

Jane wanted to stay there forever, but her stomach rumbled.

She took off, sticking her head into each room and smelling bacon frying somewhere. She'd have to figure out a way to get food.

As she sped around a corner, she ran into a huge man. He was dressed in white and his skin was as black as the night in her neighborhood.

"Whoa, Missy," said the man. "What's your hurry?"

The man had a deep voice and a strong accent. It made Jane smile.

"I'm looking for the ladies room and where I can have breakfast."

"The next door is one of the dining rooms and they will have breakfast. Also, there will be a ladies room on the left as you go in the door. Are your parents in there?"

"No," she said. "They are behind me somewhere. I ran ahead to find out where we were going."

"You may use the restroom, but you'll have to wait for them since they will have the dining pass."

Her heart sank, but she said, "Thank you" and as the man turned away she said, "Can I ask you a question?"

"Yes, Missy, how can I help?"

Jane shifted from foot to foot and finally blurted out, "where are you from?"

The man laughed. "I am from New Orleans," he said in his wonderful accent, and laughed again. "But I know what you mean. My family comes from Somalia. I came to this country when I was about your age. I am an American now and happy to be one. My name is Dalmar, what is yours?"

"My name is Isabella."

The man stuck out a massive hand. "Pleased to meet you."

She took his hand, "Likewise, Mr. Dalmar. I have to go now. My folks will be looking for me."

Actually, she had to go to the bathroom.

Real bad.

She waved to Mr. Dalmar and raced to the ladies room.

At least I'll be able to use the bathroom even if I won't eat for two days, she thought.

Jane realized that she hadn't planned well for getting food. She still had some snacks from the orphanage in her backpack, but she had to find a way to get to the food on the boat. And then, what about when she gets to Grand Isle? More starving? Maybe she could catch octopus and eat them raw.

Yuck.

Chapter Seven

A Hiding Place

After washing up and getting the remainder of the grease off her face and arms, Jane went in search of a place to spend the day where she wouldn't be easily noticed.

She wandered the boat sticking her head into different rooms. She found a ladies lounge, but it was much too fancy for her to go in. Somebody would figure out an orphan girl didn't belong there.

Then she discovered the Mark Twain room. It was like a library only about Mark Twain. She loved *Huckleberry Finn* and now she was a runaway like Huck and Jim the slave, and heading down the Mississippi—not to save herself, but another creature.

Jane glanced around as she eased into the room finding only two other people who were in a big discussion about one of Twain's books. They didn't even notice her. Jane found several of his books that she hadn't read including the *Prince and the Pauper.*

She settled into a large leather recliner. A perfect spot for the next two days. Now all she needed was a way to get food.

Around lunchtime she began to get hungry and decided to hunt for food. She prowled the passageways like a panther searching for prey.

The smell of food tickled her nose and led her to a buffet. She strode up to the person seating everyone.

"My parents are coming in a few minutes," she said. "Can I go ahead and get started?"

"No," the man replied, "families must be together. I have to see all of the meal tickets."

She thanked him, hiding her disappointment and continued her hunt. In one room she found a popcorn machine and everyone was helping themselves. So she joined in. She figured she could live on popcorn if she couldn't find any other food.

She asked a boy who was away from his parents if you could get popcorn at any time.

"Sure," he said. "But the ice cream is better. My parents only let me get it once a day."

Janes stomach rumbled. "Where is the ice cream?"

"The next deck up. On the other side, you know the starboard side."

"Thanks," she said. And took off.

Okay, she thought, now I've got popcorn and ice cream. That's a lot better than the food at the orphanage. But she still had to find a way to get real food.

After finishing the popcorn and ice cream, she moseyed back to the Mark Twain room and on the way, passed another larger dining room. She went in.

Workers were cleaning the tables and putting away the last of the buffet food. One of them looked at her and said, "We're closed now, young lady."

"That's okay," she said. "I've already eaten at a different place and I just wanted to see what you had here."

"Ask your parents, they have a menu for every restaurant each day. You just can't wander in without them."

She nodded and mumbled "grouch" under her breath and imagined the man as Snape in *Harry Potter*.

Chapter Eight

Caught

Jane took a different route back towards the small library and while walking down one deserted hallway, she found an open door to a dark room. Her eyes darted up and down the passageway and seeing no one, she went in and eased the door shut. She felt around and found a light switch and realized she was in a room with all kinds of interesting stuff.

Luggage, toys, umbrellas and more—all with tags. She finally realized this was like a lost-and-found room. Probably things people had left behind that the boat company would try to get back to them. Some had notes on them saying: "Donate." And that gave her an idea.

She studied the suitcases looking for a child size. Many were locked, but she found one, a pink one, that was open and had the note on it. Inside was some of the prettiest clothes she had ever seen. Would they fit her?

She pulled out a couple of dresses and held them up.

A bit long, but they might work. But should she take them? Since they couldn't find the owner, they were going to give them away. And they might give them to an orphanage. She was an orphan so it would be okay, but she still felt a twinge of guilt.

She slipped on a dress. It fit okay, but she'd have to check it out in the mirror in the ladies room.

Jane carefully folded her dress and put it into her backpack. She added another dress, a pair of jeans, a few blouses and shirts, two pairs of shoes, and some socks. She also took a couple of hair bows.

She hated them, but maybe they would make her look like the type of ritzy girl that would take a steamboat cruise.

She put on one of the blouses, shoes and a hair bow. Now she could strut around the boat like Fancy Nancy and maybe figure a way into a restaurant for lunch.

Jane hurried back to the rest room to check her clothes and then found a different restaurant than the "grouch" one.

She leaned against the rail watching the waiter with her eyes darting back to the open door of the restaurant.

Two women worked at the door. One checked meal tickets and the other seated people. But Jane knew, having watched for a while, that when a crowd of people arrived, both women would leave the door and seat people.

The girl waited, not so patiently, as her stomach went round and round like the paddlewheel.

Jane got ready as a crowd of eight or ten people arrived at the door. Jane got behind them and as both women left the entrance and she zoomed past the sign that said, "Wait here to be seated" and got in the buffet line.

What a feast.

Everything a hungry orphan girl could possibly want to eat. And she tried to get a little bit of everything on her plate. Roast beef, chicken, and shrimp were her first choices, but she added some vegetables and even one oyster on the half shell.

It looked nasty, but they were supposed to be good and she might never get another chance to eat one.

She also added two desserts to her tray.

She sashayed up to a table with a family of two parents and a girl about her age and an empty chair.

Jane sat her plate down and said, "May I join you? My family is such a bunch of bores."

Their mouths dropped open and they stared at her and then at her mountain of food with mashed potatoes sliding like lava onto the tray.

"I'm Isabella," she said as she sat down not waiting for them to answer. She turned to the girl next to her and said, "What's your name?"

The girl grinned at her. "I'm Emily and these are my parents."

"Pleased to meet you," said Jane as she started stuffing food into her mouth.

She had just slid the oyster into her mouth, when she realized that all three were staring at her.

She started to speak, but remembered Mrs. Dodson's manners lessons about talking with your mouth full.

Jane had the oyster in her mouth and couldn't bring herself to swallow it.

It was stuck there like a big hunk of snot slowly sliding around her mouth. Was it moving? Do oysters have feet?

She couldn't swallow it and her eyes watered.

Suddenly she gagged and gagged and spit out the oyster. It whizzed between the two adults and splatted on the floor.

The parents stared at her in horror. Emily couldn't stop giggling.

"Sorry I got choked.

"I usually have better manners, but I got up too late for breakfast and I'm starved."

The parents gave her a weak smile. Emily grinned.

Out of the corner of her eye, she noticed a large, white-dressed person coming toward her and she spun around to see Dalmar smiling at her.

"Is this your family?" asked Dalmar.

"No, they left, but I was still hungry."

Oops, she thought, I just lied about my lie.

Everybody gaped at her and Dalmar had wrinkled his brow. “Finish your meal, Missy,” he said. “And then we'll need to talk.”

Chapter Nine

Discovered!

Jane decided to get one more helping of food before she was kicked off the boat and sent to some bleak prison like Alcatraz.

On the way back to the table she watched as the family hustled out the door.

They know I'm a fake, she thought. But she sat down and ate with the watchful eyes of Dalmar on her.

When she finished, she shuffled over to Dalmar and stared up at his big brown eyes.

He motioned for her to follow him and they went to an out-of-the-way table in the back of the restaurant.

"Okay, Missy, what's going on here? You don't have family on board, do you?"

"No sir," she said with her eyes down. "I snuck on the boat."

"Why, Isabella? You know you could get in a whole mess of trouble."

"I had to.

"There is a whale, a sick whale, on the beach at Grand Isle and it's going to die if I don't get there to help it. I have to, Dalmar, I have to," she said, her words running together.

"Slow down, Missy Isabella, my English is good, but I can't understand you without a few commas and periods."

"There's a sick whale," she said with tears in her eyes.

"I know about the whale. It is a terrible thing and I saw on the news that they pulled it back into the water, but it beached again in some shallow water. The experts don't know what to do now. But how does this affect you?"

"I saw the whale on television and looked into its eye and I know that it is lonely and has no family."

She looked up at Dalmar, the tears now running down her face. "And I know what that's like. I'm an orphan. I've never had any family."

"I'm sorry, Missy Isabella, but why do you think you can help the whale?"

"Because I can feel what the whale is feeling. And

I'm sure it would be able to feel my thoughts.

"I once had a dolphin at the New Orleans aquarium tell me it wanted to be back in the ocean."

Dalmar got up and stood by the window looking at the river. Finally he said, "Are you telling me the truth?"

"Yes, sir."

"I have heard a lot of lies from you, why should I believe you this time?"

"I told all the lies so I could get to the whale. And I know it sounds stupid that I think I can talk to the whale, but I know I can. I really can."

"Tell me your whole story. Where you got on the boat and about the orphanage."

Jane explained everything.

"What did you feel when you looked at the dolphin and the whale's eye?"

"It's really strange. I didn't hear the dolphin, but I knew what it was thinking.

"And the same thing with the whale.

"I knew looking at its eye that something was wrong and it was lonely. Please believe me."

Dalmar looked at her and rubbed his chin.

"I believe you, Missy."

Jane jumped up. "Why? Nobody else would."

Dalmar got a far-away look. "When I was a boy, I lived by the sea. It was wonderful, and peaceful before the pirates came."

"Pirates?" Jane said. Her imagination took her to *Treasure Island* and she pictured Long John Silver.

"Yes, we had pirates and that's why my family left, but before them, we lived and played by the sea. I learned to love the sea creatures especially the whales that often swam by. And there was an old man who said he could talk to animals. I didn't believe him at first, but I saw it.

"Other boys and I were swimming in an area where there were rip tides. You know, the ones that can pull you out to sea. One of my friends got too close and it grabbed him and as quick as a cheetah, it dragged him way out. We boys didn't know what to do, but the old man was walking the beach and we hollered to him.

"We told him what happened.

"He squinted out to sea and then whistled. Dolphins came swimming right up and he waded out to them and made noises. They zoomed out to the boy and pushed him back to shore."

"Wow," said Jane. "I thought I was crazy and was the only person who could do that."

"You're not crazy, you're special."

Jane fidgeted and then looked up at the big man. "I saw a flyer on a bulletin board that said there is a bus tour to Grand Isle after we get to New Orleans."

She cleared her throat. "Dalmar, can you get me on the bus?"

"No, Missy. They would fire me and I need this job."

"But—the whale. I can help the whale and you said you believe me."

"I do, Missy Isabella, but I could not let you go all the way to Grand Isle by yourself even if I didn't get fired."

"I'm an orphan, I do everything by myself. I'm used to it and where I live in Baton Rouge is one of the most dangerous places a young girl can be.

"I go out all the time by myself. I have a black belt in karate."

"No Missy, you don't. You are lying again and I need you to tell me the truth. I cannot get you on the bus."

Tears again filled Jane's eyes and she looked at the floor.

She raised her head up and she stared at the large man. "I'm going to save that whale and if you don't help me, I'll figure out another way."

Dalmar sighed.

"Okay, Isabella. I will see what I can do. But don't get your hopes up. They would not let me travel with a guest, especially a girl your age. But maybe I can work something out."

"Thank you, thank you," said Jane jumping up and down. "I know you will. You'll figure something out."

"What will you do after you save the whale?"

"I don't know.

"I don't want to go back to the orphanage."

"Where will you go. You can't stay in Grand Isle."

"I'll figure something out later, but first I have to

help the whale."

Dalmar shook his head. Jane knew he was concerned about helping her, but his love for whales made the difference.

Chapter Ten

A Way to Grand Isle

A few hours later, Dalmar appeared at the door of the Twain library. His giant shadow caused Jane to look up. He motioned to her. She grinned and rushed out.

The man waited in the hallway.

"I have found a way," said Dalmar.

Jane held her breath. "Tell me, tell me."

"I found two elderly sisters, Thelma and Alice Tracy, who cruise regularly with us and I have gotten to know them well. I told them you needed to go to Grand Isle to meet some family and asked them if you can travel with them. They said yes. I hated to lie, Missy."

"Oh, Dalmar, you're wonderful, and it's okay to lie for something important. I do it all the time."

"I know," said Dalmar with a stern look.

"And that's a terrible thing to do.

"They are going to rent a car and stay in Grand Isle for two days, So you had better have a plan to go back to the orphanage by then.

"They expect your *family* to be there by the end of the two days. If this imaginary family isn't there, they will call me and I will call the orphanage."

"No, Dalmar, I can't go back. I won't."

"You have to go somewhere. You can't live on the beach or on the streets."

Jane knew he was right. She had to figure out something. But what? Tomorrow she would leave the boat with the Tracys and have two nights to save the whale and decide what to do. It was hopeless. She'd have to go back to the orphanage.

The next morning the boat moored in New Orleans. A Dixieland band greeted them and commotion was everywhere. Jane met the Traceys.

As they traveled by car to Grand Isle, Alice asked her about her family and why they weren't here. Jane had been mulling over in her mind since yesterday what lies she would tell, and she made up a sick relative that her parents had to go see. The fictional parents allowed her to stay on the boat with friends for a day, but were delayed in getting back.

Weak, she knew, but the two seemed to buy it.

The sisters were so nice and she thought about them adopting her, but they told her their life was all about traveling. They had a house up north, but only stayed there for a couple of months in the summer.

Her heart sank. She wouldn't be able to go to school. Her favorite thing after the library. Maybe they could put her in a boarding school, but that would be like being in the orphanage. Or, even better, they could home school her. That might work. But she would have to tell them the truth and she couldn't do that now. They might call the orphanage before she could help the whale.

She would ask them before they left.

Chapter Eleven

Millie

Finally, they arrived at Grand Isle.

The warm wind tickled the palm trees and the azure sea went on forever. Kids ran and played in the sand. What a wonderful place, thought Jane. She would love to just lie on the beach and read, but she couldn't. She had a mission.

The Tracy sisters had rented a small house near the beach for two days. Jane had her own room and she could see a little bit of the Gulf of Mexico from her window, but she couldn't see the whale.

She unpacked her clothes and put on shorts and a T-shirt, and asked if she could go to the beach. She had already told them that she wanted to see the whale, but didn't say anything about saving it. They wouldn't understand.

They agreed, but wanted her to meet them at the pier in about thirty minutes. Jane took off.

She carefully crossed the street and then zoomed towards the beach and the helpless whale. The path led her to a wooden pier filled with people fishing and, off to her left, she could see the animal in a small cove. People milled about it. She charged down the beach and stopped in awe when she got near the creature.

It was bigger than the van that took the orphans on trips.

Jane ran to the animal. It floated in a dug out area of the sand that had been filled with water. A white canopy covered the whale keeping the sun off and huge shower heads constantly sprayed seawater on it.

An orange fence about four feet tall kept onlookers away. Jane walked to the fence and peered at the whale. She knew it was sick—no, it was dying.

She put her hands on the top of the fence, pushed down and jumped over, then hurried to the whale. In the distance she heard a man hollering. She ignored him.

She caressed the whale's skin. The animal's eye focused on her.

"It's okay now, I'm here. I know you're a girl whale so is it okay if I call you, Millie?"

Out of the corner of her eyes, she saw two men standing at the fence. One was a red-faced guard with a gun on his hip. He pointed toward her. The other man was nodding, but staring at her and the whale.

"It's okay, Paul," the man said. "I'll go talk to her."

The man opened the gate and walked towards Jane.

"Hi," she said. "My name is Isabella, who are you?"

"My name is Carlos Rodriguez. My wife and I are the scientists in charge of trying to save this whale."

Jane stuck out her hand. "I'm glad to meet you and I'm here to help save the whale."

"And how are you going to do that?" asked the man.

"I don't know, yet, I just got here. Millie and I will have to talk for a while."

The whale's eye had not left the little girl. Its breathing seemed to have slowed.

"You know, Isabella, it's very dangerous to be this close to a huge mammal. One slight move and it could crush you."

"I know. She is so big. But she won't hurt me. Millie knows I'm here to help her."

"How do you know this is a female whale?"

"I just feel it. And I feel she is very sick, maybe dying and lonely. I need to talk to her by myself."

"I'm afraid we can't do that. It's too dangerous to have you in here. Where are your parents?"

Jane heard someone call for Isabella and she spotted Thelma and Alice coming towards her.

"Those are the people I'm staying with until my parents get here,"

"Come," said the man, "let's go talk to them."

The man opened the fence for Jane and the two went and met the Tracys. He introduced himself.

"Why were you so close to that whale?" asked Thelma. "I'm sure that's very dangerous."

"I'm sorry," said Jane. "I felt like she needed me to be there."

The sisters told her they would have to go get lunch now and that she could come back later and see the whale, but could not get close to it.

Mr. Rodriguez had said nothing during this time. His eyes darted from the whale to the girl.

Jane sighed and dropped her shoulders. She turned to the whale and said, "Millie, I'll be back soon."

And as she walked away the whale made a soft sound like a squeak. She turned to see Mr. Rodriguez jump and stare at her as she walked backwards away from the whale.

Jane smiled at Millie.

Chapter Twelve

A Conservation With Millie

That night after the women told her good night, Jane leapt out of bed. The girl had already planned to go to the whale by climbing out of the window. She wouldn't leave this early, it was just after ten, but she'd wait until after midnight and sneak out to see Millie.

She took off her pajamas and got dressed in jeans and a T-shirt and crawled back in bed. Jane decided to read using a flashlight until the clock on the dresser said midnight.

Her eyes sprang open with a start. She had fallen asleep. Jane gawked at the clock to find it was 1:15. She was late. Millie needed her now.

She had already put a jacket and a blanket from the cottage into her backpack.

She eased the window up and tossed the backpack out. This would be a lot easier than getting out of the orphanage, she thought. She went out feet first and dropped to the ground, grabbed her backpack, and headed for the beach.

No one was out, but she tried to stay in the shadows as much as possible. A sliver of moon hung low in the night and its reflection rolled with the waves. The pumps pouring water from the sea over the stranded whale broke the silence.

As the girl crept down the beach, she wondered if a giant squid lay hidden in the shallow waters waiting to grab her and drag her out to sea.

As she approached Millie, the whale made a soft sound.

She's glad to see me, thought Jane. She knows I can help and I'm probably the only one because I understand her.

Jane climbed upon the whale's fin to get closer. She didn't know if her weight would hurt the whale, but as she climbed up she felt Millie telling her it didn't hurt.

Water dribbled down the side of the whale and onto the flipper and Jane put on her jacket and wrapped herself in the blanket. She laid down on the flipper and caressed Millie.

Jane told Millie all of her adventures getting here. And what her life was like back at the orphanage. How for years every time someone came to the orphanage door she hoped they would take her to their home. But it never happened. People looking for a kid wanted a young one, not a smart aleck, older girl. Especially one that lied all the time.

Jane couldn't help herself. Her lies, her stories, were her dreams. Dreams of someday having a family and living adventures.

As she dozed and talked to Millie, she heard footsteps in the sand and glanced up to see Mr. Rodriguez and a woman standing not far away looking at Millie.

Had they seen her? Or heard her?

Jane scrunched down to make herself as small as she could be hoping they wouldn't see her hiding on the whale's fin.

The couple came closer and the man said, "Isabella, is that you up there?"

Jane raised up. "Yes, sir, it's me."

"Please come down from there."

Jane patted Millie and slid off the fin. She walked hesitantly to the man and woman.

"This is my wife, Jennifer," said the man.

"Nice to meet you, Mrs. Rodriguez," said Jane.

"Why are you here with the whale?" asked the woman.

"Don't you know it's very dangerous? And you could injure the whale by being up there on its fin."

"Millie said I wasn't hurting her and she liked having me there."

"See what I told you," said Mr. Rodriguez. "The girl believes she can communicate with the whale."

"I can. I really can. Millie has told me many things."

"I want to know why you are here without adult supervision," asked Mrs. Rodriguez.

"I'm staying with the Tracy sisters right over there," said Jane as she pointed in the direction of the cabin.

"They told me it was okay for me to come down here and stay with the whale."

"No," said Mr. Rodriguez. "I'm sure they didn't. They were very concerned about you being close to the whale yesterday and I'm sure they did not let you come down here. Tell me the truth."

Jane's head drooped. "You're right, I snuck out of the cabin and came down here. They don't know I'm here."

"Then you must get back right away," said Mrs. Rodriguez. "If they find you missing, they will call the police."

"But Millie needs me. She doesn't have much time."

"It is nearly five and the sun will be up soon," said Mr. Rodriguez. "We will be with Millie for the rest of the morning. Come back with the sisters after you've had breakfast and we will talk about Millie."

Chapter Thirteen

"I Know What To Do."

The Rodriguezes had a strange look on their faces when Jane returned. Mrs. Rodriguez put her arm around Jane.

"We're going to put her to sleep this morning. She's suffering,"

"No! Not yet."

Tears filled Jane's eyes and flowed down her face.

"We're sorry." said Mrs. Rodriguez. "But we can't let the animal suffer."

"I know what to do," Jane sniffled. "I really do."

"What do you know?" asked Mrs. Rodriguez.

"Millie is really young. She got separated from her mother right out there somewhere and she doesn't know how to get back to her. She called for her, but her voice is too weak in the air and in the water there is something else that messes up her call. I remember reading about it. Something the Navy does. I don't know what it's called."

"Sonar."

"That's it. The sonar interferes with her trying to call her mother and when you pulled her back to the ocean she got confused again because of the sonar and swam back to the beach, but I know what we can do."

The couple exchanged glances. "Tell us."

"Find a way to record her cry," said Jane, "and take it far out in the ocean and play it underwater so her mother can hear. I'm sure she's searching for Millie. And get the Navy to turn off their sonar."

The Rodriguezes again looked at each other.

"I can talk to the Navy," said Mrs. Rodriguez. "They have helped us before even if it was reluctantly."

"Maybe worth a try," said Mr. Rodriguez

"We have our recording instruments, but no aircraft," said Mr. Rodriguez.

"Maybe the Navy or Coast Guard can supply that. They might work with us if they know how big the emergency is."

"Isabella," said Mr. Rodriguez. "You know Millie won't make it through the day.

"I was ready to give her the barbiturates yesterday until you came and she rallied. We may not be able to save her no matter what we do."

"Please, sir, try. Try really hard this morning and if you can't I'll, ... I'll understand," Jane sobbed.

Mr. Rodrigues explained to her how a young animal that has recently weaned or weaned prematurely may find it difficult to fend for itself and take the wrong route due to a lack of experience. And how the sonar affects the whales. Then he squatted down and looked Jane in the eye.

"You have to tell me the truth," said Mr. Rodriguez. "Everything. Who you are. Where you came from. And how it is that you can communicate with this whale. Because I now believe you can."

Jane nodded and told her story including how she talked to the dolphin at the New Orleans aquarium.

Then she turned to Millie.

"Millie," said Jane. "I know you are very weak. But you have to try hard to call again for your mother when Mr. Rodriguez is ready.

"Then he will take your call out to the ocean so your mom can hear it. And she will come. I know she will. But you have to stay alive and I'll be here with you the whole time."

She glanced at Mr. Rodriguez. He nodded.

"You can do it Millie. I love you so much and I don't want you to die."

The Rodriguezes sprang into action. Mrs. Rodriguez decided to drive to the nearest Coast Guard station to explain the situation face-to-face.

Mr. Rodriguez made calls organizing the people who had pulled Millie out to sea the first time. He told them they had one last chance and he wanted to try it, but they had to do it first thing this morning. Time was of the essence.

Jane climbed back up on Millie's fin and began singing songs she had heard on the radio, along with hymns she remembered from the local church she sometimes attended.

"O hear us when we cry to Thee
For those in peril on the sea."

Chapter Fourteen

Saving Millie

Mr. Rodriguez returned with a microphone on a long boom with wires connected to a recording device. With Jane urging her on, Millie made a few pitiful sounding squeaks.

"That should be good enough," said the scientist.

A Coast Guard helicopter landed in a nearby parking lot and Mr. Rodriguez raced to it with his recorder and underwater microphone. He jumped aboard and the copter whisked out to sea.

Jane continued to talk and sing to Millie as she watched the helicopter stop in several places to lower the microphone until it was so far away, she couldn't see it anymore.

"Your mom will hear you I'm sure of it, Millie. Just keep breathing and she'll be here soon."

Mrs. Rodriguez and the workers pulled up in her truck and ran to the whale. "Good news, Isabella," she said with a smile.

"The organization that pulled Millie into the water before will try again. And the Coast Guard will help and they will temporarily shut down their sonar. I only hope Millie's mother will be here."

"She will," said Jane. "I know she will, but we don't have much time. Millie is real sick."

Mrs. Rodriguez ran to her truck and got a small water pump and a hose.

She told the workmen to hook it up and run the hose to a nearby outdoor faucet.

She handed the spout to Jane. "This is fresh water, not salt water, so you can spray it on her eyes without hurting her. And keep talking to her."

With clunks and grinds, a large backhoe arrived. Millie's eye strained to see what was causing the noise.

"It's okay, Millie," said Jane. "The machine is here to help you get back to your mother."

The backhoe began digging sand out behind the whale to make a passage to the sea.

"The tide is coming in and that will help float Millie," said Mrs. Rodriguez.

"Where is the helicopter?" asked Jane her voice breaking. "We have to hurry."

A tugboat appeared and waited off shore as more workmen arrived with harnesses to attach to Millie.

Jane squealed when she heard the helicopter. Mr. Rodriguez jumped out and ran to the whale. With his recording device he played a sound and Millie heard her mother. She tried to move.

"No," cried Jane, "don't move. Save your strength. Your mama is waiting for you. We'll get you back in the ocean."

The workers swarmed around Millie attaching a harness and digging out around her to allow more water to come into the small pond she was stuck in. Another group of workers laid down a special plastic behind Millie to keep her belly from scraping against the sand.

The tide rose and the channel dug by the backhoe filled with water. The tugboat came in close and attached a line to the harness. The backhoe operator tied a rope around its bucket to the harness and the workers also attached ropes to the harness.

"You have to get out of the way, Isabella," hollered Mr. Rodriguez.

"I'll be with you," Jane said to Millie, "when you get to the water."

Mr. Rodriguez yelled orders to the workers as Jane dashed away from the whale.

All the workers together tightened the ropes and Millie was dragged towards the ocean.

Jane followed still spraying water on the whale's face and mouth.

Finally, the huge animal was buoyant in the water, and the workers turned her around.

She didn't move.

Jane rushed into the sea.

Mrs. Rodriguez hollered. "Isabella, wait, you'll need a flotation device."

Jane stopped by Millie's tail and touched the whale as Mrs. Rodriguez ran to her truck and got two flotation devices and a small rubber dinghy that she hauled back down the sand. She also carried scuba gear.

Jane put on the vest.

As the tugboat pulled Millie further out, Jane paddled along side the whale and Mrs. Rodriguez followed in the dinghy.

Jane talked to Millie.

"Millie, you'll have to swim. Your mom is waiting for you. Open your mouth, Millie, you need food."

The whale didn't respond and the tugboat continued to pull the huge creature.

"Move your tail Millie," said Jane gruffly. "I mean it"

Millie's fins and tail moved slightly. Jane screamed, "You did it, Millie, You did it."

Millie took a gulp of saltwater and moved faster.

"Look, Isabella," cried Mrs. Rodriguez as she pointed out to sea.

"Spouts."

"Millie, your mother is here," squealed Jane.

The whale made a squeaking noise, then moved her flippers in an attempt to swim.

"Millie hears her mother and wants to swim to her," said Jane.

Mrs. Rodriquez grabbed her scuba gear.

She fastened on the equipment, and dived over the side with a wrench to release the harness from Millie.

The young whale slowly and steadily moved toward the blowholes still spraying water in the air.

Jane gave Millie one last hug and climbed in Mrs. Rodriguez's boat. They paddled to shore.

The girl glanced up the hill toward Mr. Rodriguez. Her heart sped up like the engines on the tug boat. At the edge of the dune stood Mr. Rodriguez and Dalmar. And beside them was Mrs. Dodson and the two sisters.

I'm doomed, she thought.

She lowered her eyes and trudged toward the adults watching her.

Chapter Fifteen

The Dream

Jane shuffled through the sand her mind racing—desperately trying to come up with a story to explain all she had done. Nothing would come. No lies, no exaggerations. Nothing. This had never happened before.

Then she realized. She couldn't lie to the group of people standing on the dune. All of them knew her lies and cared about her anyway. No matter what happened she would tell the truth.

She had to. From now on.

Jane stood with her head down in front of the adults. Mrs. Dodson rushed to her and practically hugged the life out of her. Jane guessed her ribs were broken.

"Oh my goodness girl, you sure do stink," said Mrs. Dodson.

"You should smell, Millie," said Jane. "She smells like our neighborhood when the garbage people were on their strike."

"We were so worried about you," said Mrs. Dodson. "All the girls put yellow ribbons on their beds for you."

Jane choked. She never believed that any of them liked her.

"Miss Amanda figured out where you were because of the questions you asked. I left immediately to come here."

"I'm proud of you," continued Mrs. Dodson. "I was so worried when you left, but Mr. Dalmar called the office and left a message. When I got here, I called and got the message and contacted Mr. Dalmar. He told me you were safe with the sisters and trying to save a whale. And you did it."

Jane went to Dalmar. "You knew I would need help, didn't you and yet you let me stay with Alice and Thelma until Mrs. Dodson got here while I helped Millie. Can I hug you, Dalmar?"

"You can, Missy, and can I hug you back?"

The two laughed, and as they hugged tears flowed down their faces.

"I knew you could do it Missy Isabella.

"I thought you were a whale whisperer like the man I knew when I was a boy. It is a great gift and I hope you will use it wisely."

"I will, promise."

Jane pulled herself up to her full height and looked at Mrs. Dodson. "I'm ready to go back to the orphanage now," she said.

"Well, I'd be glad to have you back, but maybe you better talk to the Rodriguezes first."

Jane jerked around to see both of them smiling at her.

Mr. Rodriguez squatted down to be at eye level with her.

"Isabella you have told us many things that aren't true —"

"Lies are what I've always done. I thought I had to because I'm an orphan," interrupted Jane.

"Then there won't be any need for you to lie again."

Jane's heart stopped. She didn't dare breathe. The sounds from the beach disappeared.

Her eyes and ears focused only on Mr. Rodriguez.

"You haven't known us long and I'm afraid we're being too forward."

Jane's throat tightened and every muscle strained. Could it be?

What she had dreamed about since she was old enough to dream.

"We would really like to adopt you and your name would be Isabella Jane Rodriquez and you would travel with us and help us with whales. Jennifer has worked as a teacher and could homeschool you. I know this is sudden and if you need time to go back to the orphanage and think about it, we'll understand."

Mrs. Dodson spoke up, "Jane, I mean Isabella, I have run a full investigation on the Rodriguezes. They are who they say they are and I can find nothing in their past that would be any danger to you. And I have a close friend, a marine biologist, who has worked with them. As a representative of the orphanage, I give my blessing if you want to be with this family."

Isabella could not speak.

Finally a "yes, sir, I would," squeaked out of her mouth.

It almost sounded like a whale voice.

Whale?

She jumped up.

"Millie. I've got to tell her."

"She's gone."

"No, she'll hear me."

And Isabella took off.

Sand spray followed her as she dashed across the beach dodging sun bathers and toddlers. The sun kissed the waves to the South and Isabella squinted.

A shadow moved away from the shore.

"Millie," she screamed. "Millie."

"I found my family, too."

Two spouts of water spurted from the sea.

The Old Cabin Mystery

One

The Mystery

A huge man stood in the shadows. On his shoulders rested what looked like a baseball bat. He turned toward Jessica. Her body tensed and she hurried past the gravel road.

At the overlook she sat down in the grass trying to relax. The sun glistened on the lake, and a soft breeze cooled her, but her hands shook. Why did that man unnerve her, she wondered.

She jumped as her uncle called for her. He had finished his work on the clogged culvert.

As she returned to her uncle's truck, she'd have to pass the gravel drive with its locked gate again.

Her shoulders tightened.

She glanced down the narrow driveway and relaxed, The man was gone.

Then a shadow moved and the giant man reappeared looking directly at her.

She ran and jumped in the truck.

"I got it cleaned out," her Uncle Ted said. "I don't know why that drain keeps clogging up. Almost as if someone was stuffing trash in there. We haven't been able to plant crops in this back field all summer because the culvert dams up the creek and floods the field. Never happened before."

He turned to her. "Sorry we had to stop. Did you have a nice walk?"

"Uh, yeah," she muttered. "Who lives down that gravel road?"

"A man called Thompson. Had a woman with him at times, but haven't seen her for a while. He's been there about a year. Stays to himself and doesn't seem to want any company. The gate you saw is always locked and he has never spoken with any of the other neighbors. I've seen him from the lake standing on his boat dock."

"Is he a huge man?"

"He looks like a decent size guy, But I wouldn't say huge. Why?"

"When I walked past the driveway, I saw a big man standing in the shadows holding a baseball bat."

"That's strange," said her uncle. "I've heard other people say they thought there was unusual goings-on down there. But folks around here mind their own business."

He gave Jessica a pointed glance and put the truck in gear.

As the old farmhouse came into view, Jessica sighed. It was exactly what she had been expecting. Boring. And she was going to spend a week here. With her goofy country cousin. Wasn't her idea. She'd rather spend a week in a medieval dungeon than on this farm in the country.

Uncle Ted pulled the truck into the driveway and her cousin, Cam, threw open the screen door. He walked toward the car with a big pie-eating grin on his face.

How that big lug could always act so happy was beyond her. Must be the water or the fresh air, but whatever it was she hoped she didn't catch it.

Aunt Tonya hugged her, and after saying hello, Cam yanked her luggage out of the trunk and carried all three pieces into the house. She followed him as he lugged her things up the steps to an attic room.

The space had a window on each end and a four-poster bed covered with a quilt against one of the windows. The whole room looked like it came out of a magazine called *Farm Life*.

Oh well, the bed did look comfortable and they were supposed to have Wi-Fi. That's the only reason she didn't argue harder about staying with her aunt and uncle while her parents went on an anniversary trip. But she sure didn't want to come to the farm with all its boring and scary stuff.

She had never stayed outside the city before and there had to be dangerous animals in the woods and fields.

Her suggestion of staying with friends brought a head shake from her parents. They wouldn't even discuss it. But as long as she could still text her friends, she could survive anything for a week. Cam set her things down and gave her another one of those goofy grins.

“You want to go with me while I feed the chickens?”

Feed the chickens? The dungeon was looking better all the time.

“No way. I’ll stay here and do some texting.” And she pulled out her phone.

“Um, you can’t.”

Jessica almost dropped her phone. “Why not?”

“There was a landslide a few miles away and it broke the cable. No Wi-Fi. It’ll take them a week or so to repair it.”

She sighed. Doomed to a week of farm follies. “Let’s go feed the chickens.”

She moped along behind him as he hefted a bag of feed and poured it into troughs for the birds. He explained how the chickens laid their eggs in the hen houses and protected them. She mentally filed the information under stuff-I-could-care-less-about. As they walked away from the chicken coop, Jessica asked, “What do you know about the people who live down the gravel road at the back of your farm?”

“Mr. Thompson? Why?”

She told him what had happened.

"A big guy with a baseball bat? That is strange."

He stopped walking.

"What?" she said feeling a twinge of nervousness.

"I was going to warn you about the lake. Well, not really the lake itself since it is a beautiful spot and—"

"Jeez," she interrupted. "What are you talking about?"

"Mr. Thompson's cabin."

"So what about it?"

Getting anything out of this boy was like trying to get a taxi at five o'clock.

"We're supposed to stay away from his cabin."

She threw her hands up in the air. "Will you please tell me the whole story. Why can't we go there?"

"I don't know. We're just not supposed to."

"There has to be a reason."

"Nobody has said. I've asked. Mom and Dad just say to leave him alone. I don't think they know for sure either. Neighbors have talked about seeing lights at night. I know there's something weird going on."

Jessica got a chill.

She knew about weird after seeing the big man, but maybe this wouldn't be such a boring week after all.

Two

The Quiet Night

Jessica snuggled down in the comfy bed. Everyone else was asleep. They went to bed at ten. Imagine that. She couldn't possibly go to sleep that early so she played games on her phone and it was now after eleven.

With no air conditioning, the attic room was stuffy and she opened the window near her bed and gulped the fresh country air. Nice, she thought.

The night was quiet and the nearly full moon lit the rolling country side.

She yawned. Maybe this wouldn't be so bad. She listened for sounds in the dark outside her window. There was no traffic noise. No sirens. No car alarms going off. Just quiet, but as she listened, she realized that the countryside was full of sounds. She heard insects and the hoo-hoo of a owl.

Then a howl echoed in the night. She sat straight up in bed.

What was that? A wolf? Or maybe a coyote?

She decided that staying inside the house at night was the best idea.

She leaned over the bed to look out the window. The moon lit the fields with a ghostlike glow. She saw a shadow move down by the barn. A wolf, or maybe just a dog? The fields looked peaceful in the moonlight, but a bit scary.

As she rested against the window sill her eyes half closed, she caught a flash of light off in the distance. Her eyes widened and she looked across the fields toward the lake and saw a light moving. It was too far away to make out what kind of light or what it was doing. She looked at the clock radio. It was after midnight.

The light brightened. Then vanished to reemerge further to her right. Something was going on down there by the lake. And she had a feeling it was near Mr. Thompson's house. She eased back in bed and pulled up the covers, but her eyes were frozen open. This place had a mystery and she was half excited and half afraid about it.

She got out of bed and slipped on her robe.

She crept downstairs trying to be as quiet as possible in an old house with squeaky floors.

In the kitchen she found the refrigerator and got a small glass of milk.

On the couch was a familiar quilt. Her mother had one just like it. She had received it from her grandmother. She was sure this quilt was done by the same grandmother. She finished her milk, wrapped up in the quilt and drifted off to sleep.

Her eyes squinted open as someone shook her. The windows showed no sign of light.

"What?" she asked.

"If you're going to sleep on the couch," said Cam, you're going to have to get up with the rest of us. We'll be turning all the lights on and Mom is starting breakfast. Do you want to go back up to your room?"

She sat up. Of course she did, she thought to herself. Nobody gets up before daylight, but then she smelled bacon frying in the kitchen.

"Maybe I'll have a little breakfast and then go back to bed."

"You can do that," said Cam. "Or you can come with me while I milk cows. Maybe you'd like to try to yourself?"

"Milk cows?" she asked. "I could hardly stand the excitement. Thanks, but I'll eat breakfast and go back to my room."

"Okay, but you might miss something." He had a mysterious grin on his face.

"What am I going to miss? Do you and the cows have something going on?"

Cam laughed. "Nope, but after milking I need to take the tractor down into the back field and drop salt blocks for the cattle."

"Oh yeah, that sounds like fun, too."

"The back field. The one that's closest to Mr. Thompson's house."

She jumped up and grinned at him. "Let me get my clothes on and I'll be ready to go."

After breakfast the two went to the milking shed and she watched as Cam milked their four cows.

He said that's all they had left and they were just keeping those cows for their own milk and butter.

After he'd loaded several salt blocks in a wagon behind the tractor, she jumped up beside him and they bounced across the fields and through several gates until she saw early morning sunlight glinting off water.

She pointed, "Is that the lake?"

He nodded.

"Where is Mr. Thompson's cabin?"

Cam pointed to her right "Over there. It's in a cove. Beautiful spot, but I'm not about to go near it."

"Aw, come on. You can stay on your property can't you? Just drive down as close as you can."

"I thought you said you were scared when you saw that man on the road."

"I was, but this is a mystery. I'd like to know what's going on."

Cam dropped off the last salt block and steered the tractor in the direction of Mr. Thompson's house. He followed a fence line that Jessica knew was the boundary. It was a taller and sturdier fence than the others and had no gates.

Cam turned toward her and opened his mouth to speak, when three gunshots echoed across the lake. His face froze and he turned the tractor around so fast that Jessica nearly fell off.

Cam mashed the accelerator and the machine leapt forward, bouncing through ruts and over rocks in a mad attempt get away from the mysterious cabin.

Three

Fishing

Cam slowed the tractor as he approached the barn. His dad stood with his hands on his hips. As Cam shut off the tractor motor, his dad said, "Son, I've never seen you drive the tractor like that. You know you could damage it."

"Sorry dad, I was down in the back field dropping off salt blocks and heard three gunshots. Spooked me."

"Why? Were you near the Thompson house?"

"Yes, sir. I got a little closer than usual."

"Were the shots fired at you?"

"I don't know. Probably not. But I got a little scared."

"Mr. Thompson is an eccentric kind of guy, but I can't believe he would shoot at you. I think it was just somebody on the lake. I know we have to mow in that area, but you need to stay out of that field closest to him as much as possible.

He glanced at Jessica.

"No more sightseeing trips," he said smiling.

"Okay, dad."

Jessica and Cam walked back to the house and sat down in the kitchen. Jessica's aunt was working in the garden.

"We really need to find out what's going on down there," said Jessica.

"No, we don't."

"Cam, listen to me. This is a real mystery. And we can figure it out."

"It might be dangerous to go anywhere near that place. I'm not completely sure those gunshots weren't for our benefit."

"Okay, maybe you're right. I've got another idea. I want you to teach me to fish."

"Fish?"

"Yeah, you know, where you put a worm on the hook and catch one of those scaly things that lives in the water."

"You're up to something."

"Well, maybe, but if we're out on the lake, we'll have a good view of his cabin.

"It might be kind of fun, boating and fishing. And we could take a picnic."

"That would be okay," said Cam. "I haven't had a chance to go fishing in forever. And since you want to do it, Dad will let me. We can go early in the morning."

Jessica cocked her head. "How early?"

Cam laughed. "I have to milk the cows first, but I can wake you up after that."

"No. I'll get up with you. We'll need binoculars."

The next morning the motor putt-putted as the boat sliced through the glass-like water while wraiths of fog drifted around them.

"The fog will burn off when the sun comes up," said Cam.

"I kind of like it. It's spooky this way."

Cam steered the boat away from the bank so as not to disturb fishermen on the shore.

He cut the engine when he was opposite Mr. Thompson's cove.

"There's too much fog to see the cabin now so we might as well fish. That's what you came for, wasn't it?"

"Yep," said Jessica. "I'll be catching those bass and swordfish and whatever else comes near."

"You might catch a bass, but it's unlikely you're going to hook a swordfish. They're ocean fish."

She lowered her lip in a fake pout. "I was counting on having a swordfish mounted in my room."

Cam shook his head and pulled out the tackle. He had grub worms he had dug out of the dirt under old moldy hay and threaded those onto their hooks. He showed her how to adjust the depth of the bait by using the cork and he told her they would just drift for a while and see if they got any bites.

He pointed out the bug spray lying in the bottom of the boat. "We'll get mosquitos when the wind slows. Repellent is a necessity out here."

Cam used a sculling paddle to propel the boat. He said that way they wouldn't scare the fish.

As they drifted in the morning quiet, Jessica jerked and pointed, "You lied to me. There are swordfish in this lake."

Cam squinted and said, "That's an alligator gar, but you're right, it does look a little like a swordfish."

"I wouldn't mind one of those guys mounted on my wall."

"We don't do sport fishing. We release any fish that we're not going to eat and gar are not good eating."

"I was kidding you, farm boy. The last thing I want in my room is a stuffed fish. But I like it that you care about the animals."

"Most farmers do. We raise and butcher animals, but we try to do it humanely."

"I don't think I could do that."

"Do you eat meat?"

"Yeah, but sometimes I wish I didn't. I hate the thought of killing cows."

Cam looked away from her and across the now clearing lake. "There's been times when I felt the same way, Jessica."

My country bumpkin cousin is much deeper than I knew, thought Jessica.

The rough wood cabin was now visible across the lake. Jessica saw a small dock with a boat tied up.

A gravel road ran down a hill to the left side of the cabin and a pickup truck was parked there. As she watched, the door of the cabin opened and a man came out. She grabbed the binoculars and Cam took her hand.

"Don't be so obvious. Get behind me and put the binoculars on my shoulder."

Jessica focused the lenses.

"He's not the man I saw on the road. And he's carrying stuff out to his boat,"

"Like what?"

"Looks like boxes of food and some camping equipment."

"He's probably going to go into the wilderness part of the lake. It's about ten miles downstream where the lake gets smaller and there are some great places to camp and fish. Dad and I did that last summer."

"That means he's going to be gone for a while."

"So, what are you thinking? As if I didn't know."

She grinned at him. "We can sneak over tonight and check out his cabin."

"No way. That's trespassing and can get you shot.

Plus, Dad said not to go near his place."

Jessica shrugged as she watched a few more minutes until Mr. Thompson got in the boat and started the outboard motor. He came out of the cove and directly toward them. She set the binoculars down in the bottom of the boat. As he passed by Cam hollered, "Morning."

The man raised his hand in greeting and smiled at them.

Cam frowned.

"What?" asked Jessica.

"He looks familiar. Maybe I have met him before, but I don't remember it."

As he disappeared in the distance, Jessica said, "He didn't look like any kind of monster. I'm pretty sure he's not a vampire, since the sun is awfully bright today. So what are you afraid of?"

"I'm not afraid," said Cam. "We just need to mind our own business."

"Okay, you can. I'm not going to pass up a chance to find out what's really going on at Mr. Thompson's."

"And how do you expect to do that?"

"I'm going to sneak in there tonight and take a look at his cabin. Can I borrow your flashlight?"

Cam chuckled. "Oh, right. The city girl is going to creep through the dark night into the woods all by herself. The first coyote call will have you back in bed in an instant."

Jessica's stomach tightened. She forgot about the animals.

"We'll see about that. I'm a lot tougher than you think and tomorrow morning I'll tell you all about Mr. Thompson's cabin."

Four

Into the Woods

Jessica's phone buzzed. She sat up, disoriented. Then she remembered where she was and what she was going to do. She shut off the alarm and dropped her head back on the pillow. Was she sure? Cam was right. She was a city girl and there would be lots of things out there in the fields and the woods that she probably wouldn't want to see.

But for some reason she thought this was important. It was more than just a mystery, there was something wrong. Mr. Thompson didn't seem like a man who would be shooting at them and have weird lights around his cabin at night, but he didn't seem like a fisherman either. He looked more like an athlete. Why would someone like him want to live alone and do nothing but fish? He apparently didn't even want company. That didn't make sense. And who was the man with the baseball bat?

I have to do this, she thought.

There's something wrong at that cabin and I'm the only one who will do anything about it.

She threw the covers off and climbed out of bed. Jessica had checked the stairs before going to bed trying to find out where to walk to keep the boards from squeaking. The outside edge seemed best. She put her feet on the edge of the steps and waddled down a step at a time. A board screeched. She sucked in a breath and waited, but nobody stirred. Jessica snuck out the door.

She rolled Cam's flashlight in her hand, but didn't turn it on. It might give her away. But if she heard nois-es ...

No, maybe she wouldn't want to know what was making the noise.

The moon winked at her as clouds floated by. The night was especially dark, and scary, when the moon vanished behind the clouds. Night noises filled the air. The clitter of insects, the whoosh of wings, and a far-away howl of a coyote.

Jessica wished she could hear a city sound, even a car alarm.

A twig snapped somewhere behind her and she spun around. Her eyes squinted into the darkness, but she saw nothing. She stared back at the house. I can do this she thought to herself.

Her heart pounded, but there was something special about being out here in the dark. The stars were amazing. She couldn't remember ever seeing them in the city and she began to relax.

There really wasn't anything out here to hurt her. The problem would be what was in the cabin. Was Thompson an ax murderer? Maybe he was insane. And maybe she was dumber than a rock for being here. But she kept going.

She climbed over the gates they had gone through before and slogged toward the strange light—the one she'd seen before and it came from where she figured the Thompson cabin would be.

She reached the boundary fence and stared at the darkness beyond. She'd have to go through the woods to get to the cabin, but she could do it.

Jessica took a deep breath and realized she had a problem. There was no gate in this fence.

She'd have to climb the fence and it had a single strand of barbed wire on the top. Oh well, she thought, I'll just have to figure it out.

She grabbed the mesh with two hands and stuck her foot into an opening. The whole fence leaned towards her and she lost her balance and fell on her back. She picked herself up and realized she would have to climb where there was a post.

The wire gave too much.

She started up the mesh at the nearest post and thought that it was going to be a breeze. It was, until she tried to get her leg over to the other side and the barbed wire caught on her jeans. She tried to shake it off, but it had stuck in the material. She was afraid to let go with one hand to get it loose. Oh, great, she thought. I may be here till morning.

She jumped as a voice whispered, "Need some help?"

Cam was on the other side of the fence and moved up beside her pulling the barbed wire from her jeans.

He helped her down.

"How did you get here?" she asked.

"I heard you leave the house so I circled around through another field. I figured you'd have a hard time getting over this fence and I wanted to be ready to catch you."

"I can take care of myself. I don't need a Prince Hayseed."

"Right. You'd have been stuck on that post until Thompson came back. Come on. Let's get this over with."

They crept through the woods and settled in behind bushes on the side of the house away from the drive. No sound broke the stillness of the night and the house appeared to be empty.

"Let's look in the window," murmured Jessica.

Cam shook his head. "I think I hear something."

What a weenie, thought Jessica, and then she heard a sound.

She grabbed Cam's arm as a glow appeared in the back of the cabin. The light brightened and she stifled a scream as a translucent apparition floated from behind the house and came directly at them.

Five

The Baseball Player

Her fingernails dug into Cam's arm as they scrunched down further into the foliage.

A man, the big man she saw, walked through the shimmering figure. She heard Cam suck in a breath. So did the man as he stopped and looked around. Seeing nothing he continued around to the front of the cabin. A light appeared inside the building as the apparition floated back behind the cabin.

"Hologram," whispered Jessica.

Cam nodded. "Supposed to scare people."

"It worked."

They watched through the window as the huge man searched the cabin. He picked one area and went over it digging through everything.

After an hour, he shut off the light and came back past them. The hologram vanished and they heard a car door close.

Jessica pointed to the cabin. Cam shook his head.

"He's still here," he whispered.

He led her away from the cabin and they climbed the fence again.

"The vehicle never left," said Cam, "The road is gravel and we would have heard it. He might be sleeping in his truck."

"Who is he?" asked Jessica. "You acted like you recognized him."

"I did. He's Bart Finley, a major league baseball player and I now know who Mr. Thompson is, too."

"What?"

"Yeah, Thompson is really Buddy Bronson who used to play for the Cincinnati Reds. Bronson and Finley were roommates, and listen to this. Thompson ... er, Bronson was charged with killing his wife. She was beaten to death with one of his autographed baseball bats in their house, but the police never could prove it, and he got off. Quit baseball and disappeared."

Jessica's mouth went dry as a desert. "A baseball bat," she whispered.

"Yeah, we now have two baseball players mixed up in the mystery."

"Wow. So Bronson has been hiding out here."

"Yeah, apparently he and his wife bought the place together under an assumed name. Probably as a get-away. Then after she was murdered, he came here to stay."

"No wonder he didn't want anyone around. And I was going to spy on a murderer."

"We were lucky he wasn't here, but he didn't seem dangerous when we saw him in his boat and what was Finley doing?"

"Searching. But for what? He's taking one part of the cabin at a time and going over it with a fine tooth comb. It has to be something awfully important and something he doesn't want Bronson to know about. Maybe Finley was the murderer."

"I thought about that, but the police couldn't find any fingerprints or other forensic evidence in the house. Nobody's but Bronson's."

"I think Bronson is innocent and I've got a strong hunch that Finley did it."

"Is that something city girls can do—solve crimes?"

"City girls can do anything."

Cam laughed. "Come on. It's light in the east and Mom and Dad will be up. We need to be in the barn milking cows so they won't know we've been up all night."

As Cam milked the cows, Jessica asked, "Is there some way we can watch that gravel road to see if there's a car parked beside the house?"

"Yes. We could go through the back field close to where you and Dad stopped, climb the fence and come onto the road above the cabin. But I don't have time to do that. I've got work and there's nothing I know of that needs to be done in the back field, so no reason to go there."

"Make something up. This is a farm, right? I'm sure there's always something that needs work."

"I can't lie to my dad."

"Why not?"

"Because he's my dad."

"Well, I'll tell you what, Mr. Boy Scout. I'll lie for both of us."

"How did you know I was a Scout?"

"OMG. You really are."

"I'm not too involved anymore. Too busy. But it's a great organization."

"And you probably had your own pet cow?"

"Lamb."

"Oh no, I can't stand it. I'm stuck in an old black-and-white movie."

"I always liked those. It's *A Wonderful Life* was my favorite."

"Of course it was. You're putting me on, huh?"

"Maybe a little, but, okay, when do you want to check the cabin?"

"Let's go in the daytime."

"What are you going to do? Break into the house?"

"Sure, why not?"

"Because it's against the law."

"I know that, but so is murder. And if I'm right and Finley did it, then we can figure it out."

"I know, city girls can do anything."

"You're getting there."

"But, no, we're not breaking into Mr. Thompson's house."

"All right, don't lie to your dad, and we won't break

into the house, but let's at least go down and check it out. We can probably learn a lot by looking through the windows."

"Okay, but I've got to have a real reason for going into the back field, but I'll figure something out."

Six

Into the Cabin

That afternoon they drove the tractor to the east field where Cam mowed a section of grass that was barely high enough to cut. He parked the tractor and they climbed the fence and snuck through the woods. At the road they could see the cabin at the bottom of the hill. There was no car.

"Let's go down." Jessica said

"Okay, but we'll go back to the tractor and drive it over there. Just in case we have to make a fast escape."

At the cabin they walked around looking in windows and making sure they couldn't be seen by anyone from the water. Nothing seemed out of place.

"We gotta go in," Jessica said.

"No."

"We have to. Somebody killed Mr. Bronson's wife and I know it was Finley. We just have to prove it."

"How?"

"By finding what he's looking for."

"We don't even know what he's looking for, and if he can't find it knowing what it is, how can we?" asked Cam.

"Because we're smarter. Let's think about it. If Finley really did kill Mrs. Bronson in her own house then why would he do that? It has to be she knew something about him. Was there a love triangle going on?"

Cam shook his head. "There was never any talk about Finley or Bronson's wife getting involved with somebody else. And I'm sure the police investigated."

"So maybe nothing happened. Maybe Finley or Mrs. Bronson just thought something had happened. Maybe it was blackmail."

"That is interesting," said Cam. "It could be that Mrs. Bronson had something on Finley. That would give him a good reason to kill her and blame it on her husband. But what did she have?"

Cam rubbed his chin and answered his own question. "A letter."

"Nobody sends letters anymore."

"My mom does, and both of these guys came from small towns in Ohio. That's why they roomed together."

"Okay, maybe you're right. So he wrote a letter that had something incriminating in it. He wanted it back, but she wouldn't give it to him. But how does he know it's here?"

"No idea, but she must have given him some indication before he beat her to death."

"What a sicko. I'd like to get my hands on him."

"Oh, yeah. Finley is a two hundred and fifty pound athlete and you're going take him on."

"City girls can do anything."

Cam rolled his eyes. "This goes against my better judgement, but let's check the windows. And remember. Bronson, not Finley, may be the murderer. We're just guessing here."

Jessica punched him on the shoulder and tried the nearest one. It was locked, as were all the others.

She slumped to the ground. "Now what?"

"It's time for a farm boy to go to work."

Cam took out his pen knife and slid the blade between the upper and lower windows. It caught on the latch and he twisted the blade. The latch popped open.

"Good work," said Jessica as she jumped up.

"Farm boys can do anything," he said.

She laughed.

He opened the window and hesitated.

"What's the matter?"

"I thought I heard something. Let's check."

They circled the cabin and found nothing. No boats at the dock and no cars in the drive.

"False alarm, I guess," said Cam.

The sun had sunk into the trees as they went back to the window and Cam climbed in first.

"Watch out here," and he pointed to a small nail sticking out.

He helped Jessica in and they both stood in a tiny kitchen with a small eating table and a refrigerator and stove.

"Not much in this room," said Cam. "Where does the smart city girl want to look?"

"If it is a letter," she replied. "And that makes a lot of sense, where would she put it? And why can't Finley find it?"

She snapped her fingers. "It's in plain sight!"

"*The Purloined Letter*," he said.

"You've read Poe?" she asked.

"Yeah, you too?"

"Of course. Let's hope Mrs. B did."

"We have a lot in common," said Cam.

"Um, I usually don't have manure on *my* shoes."

Cam chuckled.

Jessica led into the living room and she stopped short, holding her breath. In the corner was a baseball bat.

"Look," she whispered to Cam.

He nodded and pointed to a stack of envelopes on a table in the living room, but they were all recent bills.

On the wall was a wooden letter holder with three pockets. Magazines were stuffed into two of the openings and the other had envelopes.

Jessica pulled out the letters. They were renewal requests for magazines. *National Geographic, Field and Stream*, and *Outside.*

All had been opened and were long past the renewal date. As Jessica carefully put them back, she hesitated. The National Geographic envelope felt thicker than the others.

As she took it back out, they heard a twig snap outside the front door.

"Somebody's here," hissed Cam.

She stuffed the letter back and ran for the kitchen. Cam went through the window first and took her arms to pull her through. Her jeans snagged on the exposed nail. As she struggled to free herself, she heard the door creak open. She glanced back to see a shadow moving toward the kitchen.

A shadow carrying a baseball bat.

Seven

The Letter

"What are you doing in my house?"

The man she saw on the lake that she now knew was Buddy Bronson stood in the kitchen doorway holding a baseball bat.

Cam stuck his head into the house. "Mr. Bronson. I'm Cameron Barnes from the farm behind you. We mean you no harm. I'll come in the front door and explain everything."

Jessica eased back into the room as the nail slid out of her jeans. She stared at the large man with a grim look on his face and a baseball bat resting on his shoulder.

Her heart tried to escape her rib cage.

"Into the living room," he ordered.

She sat on the sofa and Cam came in and joined her.

"Tell me why you're in my house and it better be good. And how do you know who I am."

"I'm really sorry, Mr. Bronson," said Cam. "We never should have done this. Our imaginations got carried away."

"No," said Jessica. "We saw your friend Bart Finley searching your house and wondered what he was looking for. I think he killed your wife."

"What?" said the man. "Bart Finley is one of my best friends. He has a key to this place and takes care of it when I'm gone. You kids are in big trouble. I'm going to turn you over to the police."

Cam glared at Jessica. "Don't call the police, Mr. Bronson. We didn't mean any harm and we didn't steal anything."

"I know this isn't the first time you've been in here. I saw you watching me out on the lake and I'd found some of my things moved, so I watched the cabin from the far side of the lake. I saw you snooping around today. I sculled across the lake so you wouldn't hear me."

"This is the first time," Jessica said. "Finley has been searching your house, not us. We saw him last night digging through drawers.

"And we know what he was looking for."

"That's the dumbest excuse I've ever heard for theft," said Bronson.

He took out his cell phone.

Jessica gritted her teeth. "I can prove it," she blurted.

Cam and Mr. Bronson both stared at her.

"There's a letter from Finley to your wife hidden in this room and I know where it is."

Cam looked at her with wide eyes.

"Show me," said the man.

Jessica's mouth went dry.

Please be there, she thought as she went to the letter holder. She retrieved the *National Geographic* mailing and took it to Bronson.

"This is only my *National Geographic* renewal," he said with a scowl. "I never got around to renewing it. Edith always did that for me."

Tears welled up in his eyes.

"Look inside," said Jessica.

He pulled out the pre-paid renewal envelope and shrugged his shoulders.

"Inside that."

The man opened the envelope to find a letter addressed to Edith Bronson, his wife.

Bronson scrunched up his face. "This can't be."

Jessica let out a long, slow breath.

He opened the letter and began to read, "My dearest Edith. Since you refuse to talk to me, I'm writing you this —"

"I'll take that," interrupted a booming voice.

Jessica jumped. A huge man stood in the outside doorway with a pistol pointing at them. It was Finley.

"Thank you for finding it for me, little lady," said the baseball player.

"Bart," said Bronson. "What's going on?"

"The girl knows. She figured it out. I knew I heard something last night, so I parked my truck at the overlook and saw you two check the cabin from the road. I've been watching you ever since."

Bronson's face turned red. "You killed Edith. You. My friend. I trusted you."

"I didn't want to, but I had no choice. I loved her. More than you ever could, but she never responded. When I told her, she'd make a joke about it.

"Said she only loved you. I didn't believe her. I knew I could persuade her to leave you, but then she refused to answer my calls and wouldn't open the door. So I wrote her this letter. Stupid of me because she never wrote back.

"I went to your house and forced my way in. She was furious and tried to call the police. I couldn't let her do that, could I? Then I saw your bat mounted on the wall. It gave me an idea. I could kill her and you'd get the blame, but the problem was the letter.

"I threatened her with the bat and demanded she tell me where it was. She said after she got it she was afraid I'd do something crazy and she hid it where she knew you'd find it, Buddy.

"I knew she loved this cabin and I asked her if it was here. She said no, but I saw her eyes and knew she was lying. Then I killed her."

Jessica sniffed and wiped a tear. "She hid it in the National Geographic renewal because she knew you'd renew, Mr. Bronson, but you never did."

She turned to Finley. "And why didn't the police find evidence you were in the house?"

"I made sure they wouldn't," said Finley. "I wiped down everything I touched and vacuumed everywhere I went. I left no trace so it would be blamed on Buddy."

"Why, Bart? We were friends."

"I was never your friend. I wanted your wife and your starting position on the team. I found out I couldn't have her, but I'm the star player now."

"You won't get away with this, Bart. There are three witnesses now."

"There won't be," said the man, his voice cold.

Eight

The Boat Ride

Jessica's breath stopped. She looked at Cam and saw his clenched fists. They had to do something.

The man took their cell phones, picked up the bat, and said, "Let's go. Out to the boat."

Finley got in the boat first and sat at the bow. He ordered the two cousins in next and told them to lie down on the bottom of the boat just past the motor. Then Bronson got in and he was told to drive the boat.

Cam and Jessica got on their hands and knees, but the man ordered them to lie down flat. Jessica stretched out and something jabbed her in the ribs. She rolled over and saw a can of bug spray. She moved it out of the way and clutched it in her hand.

The boat left the cove and traveled into the main lake, its destination the wilderness area several miles away.

It was going to be the longest trip in Jessica's life.

An hour later they floated into a small, empty cove.

Rocks and ledges filled the bank and a faint trail led out of the cove.

Finley ordered Mr. Bronson to shut off the engine. The boat drifted in utter quiet. Nobody said a word. Finally the man smirked and said, "Who's first?"

Jessica held up her hand and said, "Me. City girls are always first."

"Good," the man said. "You were the nosey one. I knew you'd be trouble when I saw you on the road that morning."

"Don't do this, Bart," said Bronson. "Kill me, but let the kids go. They'll swear not to say anything."

Finley laughed. He picked up the bat in one hand while pointing the gun at Jessica. "You're going to have a terrible boating accident and hit your heads on the rocks. Come closer girl detective."

Jessica pulled herself up with her left hand on the seat. Her right hand held the can of bug spray out of sight of the man. She glanced at Cam.

She knew he understood. She swung her left leg over the seat straddling the narrow board and keeping her right hand behind her,

"That's far enough," the man said.

Cam moved and coughed loudly. The man's eyes momentarily left Jessica and she raised the bug spray and blasted him in the face. The man screamed and pulled the trigger. The bullet whizzed past her ear. Cam pounced, leaping over the seat and grabbing the gun with both hands. Cam was strong, but the man was stronger and he wouldn't let go of the weapon. Finley dropped the bat and wrapped his free arm around Cam's neck. Jessica snatched the sculling paddle and hit Finley's head full force with the edge of the paddle. He hollered and she hit him again.

Bronson grabbed the man's arm and Cam wrestled the gun out of his hand. The boy stepped back pointing it directly at Finley's chest.

"Don't move. Don't even breathe. I've been killing varmints since I was a kid and I never really liked it, but you I wouldn't care."

"Take it easy, son," said Bronson. "I wouldn't mind killing him myself, but he'll go to jail for the rest of his life.

"Let's get him back to the house."

Bronson dug out a coil of rope from a tackle box and forced the man to the bottom of the boat. He tied his hands and feet together.

Jessica remembered little about the trip back across the lake. All she did was stare at the man who had tried to kill her.

It all made sense now. The clogged up culvert, the light in the distance, the gunshots, and Finley staring at her from the gravel road. All planned to keep anyone away from the cabin until he found the letter.

At the cabin they retrieved their cell phones and called the police. The state police and the sheriff arrived and took the man away.

The two cousins flopped down on the couch in Mr. Bronson's living room completely exhausted.

Cam leaned over and smiled at Jessica, "Okay," he said, "I'm a believer. City girls really can do anything."

She grinned back at him, "And so can farm boys."

Author Notes

A special thanks to the children of Ekron Elementary for their story ideas. I loved visiting their school and writing stories together. Some of them are in this book.

Also, a shout out to the Kentucky Reading Project teachers attending my training session at Kentucky State University. A few of the stories we wrote during the training are in this book. Their stories and my information on writing for children can be found in the book *Tales for Kids*.

Books By Ben Woodard

A Stairway To Danger
Shakertown Adventure Book 1
Young adult novel.

Steps Into Darkness
Shakertown Adventure Book 2
Young adult novel.

The Staircase of Fire
Shakertown Adventure Book 3
Young adult novel.

The Boy Who Flew With Eagles
Middle grade short novel

Bubbles: Big Stink in Frog Pond
Children's picture book

A Problem With Donuts
Children's picture/activity book

Whispers of Trees
Middle grade short novel

Found in bookstores and online stores.

Made in the USA
Middletown, DE
02 September 2021